THE LEGACY SERIES

SERIES TITLES

Neon Steel
Jennifer Maritza McCauley

How We Do Things Here
Matt Cashion

Release of Information
Kali White VanBaale

The Divide
Evan Morgan Williams

Yes, No, I Don't Know
Kathryn Gahl

The Price of Their Toys
John Loonam

The Caged Man
Calvin Mills

A Day Doesn't Go By When I Don't Have Regrets
J. Malcolm Garcia

These Are My People
Steve Fox

We Should Be Somewhere by Now
Stephen Tuttle

Burner and Other Stories
Katrina Denza

The Plan of Chicago
Barry Pearce

Trust Issues
K.P. Davis

Adult Children
Laurence Klavan

Guardians & Saints
Diane Josefowicz

Western Terminus: Stories and A Novella
Michael Keefe

Jennifer Maritza McCauley's *Neon Steel* is a personal and insightful look at what it means to live and ultimately thrive in a space of "in-betweeness," as a both a Black and Puerto Rican person, a Black nerd (or "Blerd"), and as a person growing up in the days of AOL Messenger, on the verge of the future, but still tethered to the past. As so many Black kids have done, these characters discover themselves through mediums that celebrate in-betweenness, anime, tabletop games, and arcade life. In these worlds, a person can be both "normal" and powerful, human and superhuman, fitting in but extraordinary. *Neon Steel* asks readers to take a second look at "Blerd" life and ask is it just about being nerdy, or is it about self-discovery? Odds are you will find people similar to the characters in this work, people who want to own their true selves but are still finding the language for that task. Creating that language is a defiant act in a society that desperately wants Black people to be only one, digesitble thing.

—MONIQUE L. JONES
author of *The Book of Awesome Black Americans*

Jennifer Maritza McCauley's *Neon Steel* is a hybrid masterwork that's equal parts autofiction, bildungsromane, flash narrative, Pittsburgalia, and interstitial, multi-modal paean to Black nerd culture. More akin to a season of Japanese anime (complete with linked episodes and standalone OVAs!) than it is a cookie-cutter coming of age tale, McCauley's writing is vulnerable, relatable, heartfelt, and capable of moving from magical flights of high fantasy to the deepest pathos in a single paragraph. The result is a book that tells the story of a Pittsburgh that's hardly ever mentioned, let alone celebrated, from the perspective of those who are often left out, if not forced from, the public eye. Ultimately, *Neon Steel* is the book our greater American culture needs and deserves right now, for it places our feelings of estrangement and outsiderism right where they belong: squarely at the forefront of the conversation. In two simple words, "Buy it!"

—RONE SHAVERS
author of *Silverfish*

NEON STEEL

stories

Jennifer Maritza McCauley

CORNERSTONE PRESS
UNIVERSITY OF WISCONSIN-STEVENS POINT

Cornerstone Press, Stevens Point, Wisconsin 54481
Copyright © 2026 Jennifer Maritza McCauley
www.uwsp.edu/cornerstone

Printed in the United States of America.

Library of Congress Control Number: 2026930398
ISBN: 978-1-968148-23-2

Cornerstone Press titles are produced in courses and internships offered by the Department of English at the University of Wisconsin–Stevens Point.

DIRECTOR & PUBLISHER
Dr. Ross K. Tangedal

EXECUTIVE EDITORS
Jeff Snowbarger, Freesia McKee

EDITORIAL DIRECTOR
Brett Hill

SENIOR EDITORS
Paige Biever, Ellie Atkinson

PRESS STAFF
Allison Lange, Samantha Bjork, Sophie McPherson, Andrew Bryant, McKenna Bartel, John Evans, Gwen Goetter, Brian Grzesik, Kim Janesch, Ryleigh Miller, Sam Zajkowski

To Abba, my family, and little Jennie.

ALSO BY JENNIFER MARITZA McCAULEY:

Kinds of Grace
When Trying to Return Home
SCAR ON/SCAR OFF

EPISODES

The creative writer does the same as the child at play; he creates a world of fantasy which he takes very seriously.
—Sigmund Freud

0

Online

AOL INSTANT MESSENGER

MidnightWanderer477: Hey

MidnightWanderer477: Hi!! I just wanted to introduce myself. I'm Midnight and I've been reading the shounen and shojo parodies on your site every week. The gundam wing one was SO FUNNY. Hiro's hair is really spikey… you're right!

MidnightWanderer477: Hey

PlanetSenshi191: U really reading it?

MidnightWanderer477: YES

PlanetSenshi191: Nice

MidnightWanderer477: Thanks for responding! Your site is very cool.

PlanetSenshi191: Thanks, you. I'm glad someone cares.

MidnightWanderer477: What do you mean?

PlanetSenshi191: The trolls got to it and I was planning to just shut it down tomorrow.

MidnightWanderer477: OH NO

PlanetSenshi191: Yeah

MidnightWanderer477: Please don't. PLEASE

PlanetSenshi191: I dunno. I'm still thinking about it. I'm not very popular at my school already so I don't want to get my self esteem gutted everyday.

MidnightWanderer477: PLEASE keep it up. I'm not popular either. In fact my Dad's never around and my mom is always fighting with him and I look forward to your parodies every week to get me through stuff and and

MidnightWanderer477: HELLO

MidnightWanderer477: Sorry if I shared too much!!

PlanetSenshi191: No. I feel like you. Stop saying sorry. Be like Sailor Jupiter, always tough and ready to fight. "I'll make you feel so much regret, it'll leave you numb! I am the Pretty Guardian who fights for Love and Courage!"
MidnightWanderer477: I bet you're really cool in real life!

PlanetSenshi191: I am but only in my own head. Everyone at my school thinks I'm a loser.

MidnightWanderer477: Mine too. But at least we can connect here!

PlanetSenshi191: Yeah

MidnightWanderer477: What will your next parody be?
Planet Senshi191: Dunno. What u think I should do? I did too many sailor moons and yu yu hakushos

MidnightWanderer477: Maybe Revolutionary Girl Utena! Because Utena is going to become a prince herself! That's what we can do!! Become princes ourselves!!

PlanetSenshi191: OK. I'll do it

MidnightWanderer477: Yay! YAY!!

PlanetSenshi191: Only for you

MidnightWanderer477: WOOHOO

PlanetSenshi191: OK u can calm down

MidnightWanderer477: *breathes* OK OK

PlanetSenshi191: Hey

MidnightWanderer477: Yeah???

PlanetSenshi191: thxxx friend

MidnightWanderer477: ?????

PlanetSenshi191: Nm

1

The Girl in the Bomba Dress

Adrienne was late. She hated being late, but here she was, late for Algebra II, and she wasn't going to embarrass herself in front of all those white kids. What would they say? Dumb girl from Sharpsburg, of course, she's nothing. Or their eyes would do all the gibbering. Pin-points and spitfire, that's what they'd give her. Who cared either way?

She ran from her place on Chapman Street, fast, faster than she normally ran, her backpack slamming up and down on her little back and causing her red pain. As she was running past trash-thick cans and darkened bars and new coffee shops bright and yanking folks in for heavy caffeine, she thought about how all she needed to do was get to homeroom. She could be quiet. Nobody would notice her if she blended in and said nothing. She just had to get there. They all knew her, after all she was the only Black girl in the school outside of Tyana, and they knew Adri as the one who Always Did School Right. But here she was late. Per usual.

Halfway through Adri's sprint down the high-stacked rust-red buildings she heard a grunt. It was a woman's grunt, and it was stark enough that Adri stopped in her tracks, thinking someone was hurt. She turned around and approached the alley behind her, black and garbage-filled, the cans drooping with shit and pizza.

She walked past the alleyway, toward an opening flanked by a wall of graffitied brick. A mural of Black folks wearing purple, looking royal, smothered the alleyway.

In the center of the open space, there was a young woman, a little older, but not much more than Adri's sixteen years. She had long hair in fluffing curls. She wore an ivory dress that crimped and flew as she danced. Her eyes were closed. She was meditating, meditating, her muscles tensing, tensing. She sang *Bámbula, Bámbula.* Adri stared at this girl, not knowing exactly what to say, and while she was trying to gauge how fast she should run to class, the girl's eyes snapped open, and she saw Adri.

"Who are you?" she said.

"What?" Adri whispered. She could tell this bomba girl was beautiful, her body bronzed and blazing. The bomba girl could be a terrifying stranger, but Adri felt soft around this girl. What was she doing in an alley in the middle of Pittsburgh of all places?

"Where are you going?" the bomba girl asked gently, her voice deeper than whatever young age she was.

"To school," Adri gulped. "Aren't you in school?"

"No," she said. "I work deep in the night. I practice bomba in the day, preparing myself."

"For what?"

She turned back to her swishing work, spread her hands out; she shook them. The bangles on her wrists clanged and clacked.

"You do this without drums?" Adrienne asked. Her family in Puerto Rico would Bomba sometimes, she knew you couldn't flail and shake without a good beat.

She pressed her hand against her chest. "It's in here."

"I don't believe that."

"That's very American. To be so cynical."

Adrienne shrugged. "Girl, I'm a junior. I'm just trying to get into college."

She smiled, a half-grin and went back to the quick work of moving her hands about.

"Okay," she said, in that unnervingly dark voice and Adrienne didn't know what to do with her. "That's your path."

"This is a sacred art," Adrienne opined. "Why do you do it?

"Girl," she mimicked Adrienne and swept her hands out. "Aren't *you* a sacred art?" Adrienne's face said "WTF," and it was true; she didn't value herself at all. She was just a high school girl from Sharpsburg with nothing to her name, but a bunch of slurs hurled at her face and here was this gorgeous girl talking about how she was something beautiful.

"I guess I am."

"Say it with your chest, mami."

"I want to do what you do, freely," she said. Then she said it with her chest, another cliché: "Puedo hacer cualquier cosa…"

"O le se," she tried, in a language Adri didn't know and as she spun around, Adrienne saw her own face in her spinning. "There you go," she said gently. She stopped dancing and came over and tugged at the belt around her waist. "Me quiero tal como soy…"

She reached out and clutched her hands. Adrienne remembered she had homeroom but as she gripped her heated fingers back, she suddenly didn't care. They could say what they wanted. She stretched her back and Adri stretched hers. They were dancing, dancing, dancing African-Boricua music, taking them to palm tree'd places they'd never been, in Pittsburgh's aching center, not worried about the time.

2

Afro Otaku

I hadn't been back to The Mills—a brown-flushed, abandoned mall atop the crooked elbow of Blawnox mountain—since I'd graduated from high school. My gap year after my time at Fox Chapel had been largely a bust. I'd been to college for a semester, dropped out, worked a few odds jobs then ran out of money after the Oakmont caregiving company I worked for went under. I moved back home with my parents and eventually enrolled in the University of Pittsburgh.

Since I lived with my parents, my friends were few. I tried starting up conversations in class but the students largely stuck in friend-clusters and stayed to themselves. My first month in school was fine; I studied, I answered questions, I returned home. Nothing large nor grandiose to report. I had one girlfriend who moved away, one penpal and some online friends. I'd never had a boyfriend though I dreamed of the experience. I read shojo manga every night and imagined my own Yuu Matsuura would come and enliven my insipid days at Pitt.

He didn't.

I was vastly lonely. My parents constantly fought at home, my mother even threatened to go back to Puerto Rico. I couldn't concentrate on my schoolwork so I had to spend my days at Laurie Anne West, gobbling up fictional worlds and comic book panels. I was a solitary nerd, my high school friends, fellow social outcasts had gone to various other colleges, and I was the only one left in Pittsburgh.

One day on campus, I saw a poster for Anime World, a new store opening at the Mills. It was about ten minutes from me in O'Hara, where my parents lived, and I nearly salivated thinking about the new issues of manga I would buy and how convenient the place was to me. I borrowed my Mami's taupe Subaru and drove up to the Mills, excited for the little snatch of escapism within my grasp.

When I entered the once flourishing-mall, I was immediately taken by its emptiness. A rush of dead air struck me when I walked through the sliding doors. There were Borders that used to be thriving and a Waldenbooks that used to compete with the Borders, and there was a Rue 21 and a Macy's and JCPenney, all flashing staples of commercialism now whisked away. The only stores remaining were mom-and-pop places, the arcade, a Christmas shop that stayed open all year and a place that sold terrifying baby dolls.

And now apparently Anime World.

Anime World was also barren but stocked with cosplay costumes, shelves of pristine, glaze-faced manga, and the best line up of anime DVDs and used VHSs I had seen in some time. They had the full seasons *of Neon Genesis Evangelion, Outlaw Star, Nadia Secret of the Blue Water,* and *Trigun.* They even had a nice stack of OAVs, even the new *RurouKen* OAVs which had ruined the series for me after Kenshin died at the end. I was shaking with joy, feeling as if I'd happened upon a kind new neon-fringed riches.

As I was pondering these things, I felt a shadow approach me. It was a man, tall, bronzed and simultaneously lanky and soft-bodied, with dark curls greased against his head. He wore a blue and yellow plaid shirt and a tag with his name: Benedict. I was, as always, happy to see another Black person out in the Pittsburgh 'burbs. He grinned and plucked his thumb at a DVD copy of *Vampire Hunter*. I noticed he had long, pianoman fingers.

"Looking for anything special?" he asked.

I blurted out, against my better judgment,

"Do you really like anime?" as if I had found an oasis in a desert.

He chuckled. "Of course." He rolled his shirt up to his elbows to reveal a tattoo of Ranma in his boy form. "Also, I work here."

"Rumiko Takahashi," I gushed. "My favorite."

"Mine too," he said, as if it were the most obvious thing. "So what are we looking for today? *Maison Ikkoku? InuYasha?*"

I blushed. "I don't know yet. I have to check it out." I had never met a Black otaku before and I was caught off guard. He and I started chatting about anime and manga and the more we talked the more my pulse fired off and intensified. As a girl who had dreamed of having a boyfriend but could never get a guy to come up to me, fresh happiness hit me in my bones. I felt like a shojo manga was coming alive before my eyes and I didn't know how to react. I tried not to get too excited.

"You seem like you've never seen a Blerd before." He smiled. "Where are you from?"

"Outside of the city. It's pretty white."

"There are tons of Blerds in the city. In fact I have a group that hangs out in the arcade on the other side of this mall during the summer. If you want…" He said the last part sheepishly as if he didn't know if I'd come.

"I'm there!" I said, and almost kicked myself for being too enthusiastic.

I hung around the store until Benedict finished his shift and ended up buying way more manga than I had originally anticipated. The small, glossy books leaped around in my bag as I followed Benedict from his shift to the other side of the abandoned mall.

Along the way he told me about himself. His mother was Black American and his father was Latino and was absent most of his life but had come back to Pittsburgh recently after an illness. His father was from Some Island but Benedict didn't know where. He lived in Homestead and commuted all the way over to the Mills for this job because he loved the arcade and Anime World so much.

He explained, "I'm like anime-adjacent. I watch it, I know it, but I'm more of a *Dance Dance Revolution* kind of guy." At this I brightened. Some of my friends in high school liked *Dance Dance Revolution* too. "I can't wait to see you dance," I said and almost bit back the phrase. He chuckled and switched his eyes at me. "If you hang with us you can go to my competitions."

"I'd love to!"

By the time we reached the arcade, I was sweating with excitement and joy. He raised a hand at the cashier in front and led me behind rows of empty *Mario Brothers, Pac-Man* and *Street Fighter.*

"It's not the most popular spot," he said. "In fact, no place in this mall is. You were our first customer all day."

I raised my eyebrows. I hoped Anime World would keep existing months from now. He led me behind the *Dance Dance Revolution* machine and gestured toward it.

"That's my passion," he said.

"So cool," I said.

He grinned small and led me through the dark back-room, with smudges on the blue walls and a grime-specked floor. I heard percolating conversation and random spurts of Japanese. He kicked a very tightly closed door open and it was full of a wide assortment of folks. The first person I saw was a trans Asian man with perky breasts, jean shorts and earrings that had images of glittering dragons. The Asian kid had a headset on and was playing bootlegged *Dragon Ball GT* on PlayStation on a large TV screen. He yowled and roared. The walls were adorned with posters of *Dragon Ball Z, Sailor Moon, Kingdom Hearts, Hunter x Hunter, Berserk, Video Girl Ai*, and *Final Fantasy* along with shelves of anime and manga. A very short Black woman—probably 4'10, with purple twists styled after the anime girl in *Neon Steel* bounced up and down on another bean bag chair and talked excitedly to a young guy with a huge Afro who was playing a paper RPG.

Benedict held open the door with his long body and put a hand on my shoulder.

"Hi everyone. This is Adrienne-chan. She's new to the Mills. She's an anime girl."

The girl with twists piped up "Ooh, just like me. Is she your crush, Benedict?"

He blushed and waved her away. "That's Elana. She's really into *Final Fantasy*." She waved her mittened hands.

He gestured toward the Asian kid. "That's Godai. Or rather Dragon217. He's into *Dungeons and Dragon*s and hates anime."

"Despise it," Dragon217 said. "But I'll get you anything you want from back home. I actually do scanlations for a few websites to pay for classes. We've got you covered, Adrienne."

My pulse sped up. I was meeting folks who actually did the bootleg translations I read online. "Of course! That's so kind of you. I actually got my anime bootlegged when I first started. The VHS fansubs straight from Japan."

Dragon217 grinned. "Yeah, that's the shit. If you like anime."

Benedict gestured to the Afro'd kid on the bean bag chair. He looked up, his eyes rolling about to and fro. "I'm Ferris. I like anime the most. You'll have to beat me."

"He's kind of a mastermind," Benedict explained. "Good at everything."

"Hey," I joked, just overjoyed to see everyone. "I was president of the anime club in high school."

"Heavily bullied?" Ferris smirked.

"Hell yeah."

He raised a thumb. "She's definitely one of us. Don't worry we were all outcasts when we were young."

I scanned the place. It felt glossy, shiny, exciting, new. "So you guys just hang out here?"

"We're all college students, from Point Park, Pitt, Carlow and CMU," Ferris said. "We used to meet at CMU but once Anime World and the arcade opened we decided to move it. We meet here during the summers. It's pretty fun. Sit down."

He gestured to one of the bean bags and I plopped down. Benedict stayed standing, his arms folded. I noticed the lines of his forearm muscles, and I found it strange that I was so attracted to that part of his lovely body.

"So," he said. "I'm going to my last DDR competition at Dave & Buster's in Homestead. Some of the group are coming. You're definitely invited," he said the last part carefully.

"Sure," I said, trying to make myself seem interesting now that I was around my new friends. I couldn't hold it for long. "I mean, of course! That sounds amazing!"

He gave me a slow high five and I left my hand on his large hand. I swallowed big and he retracted his hand. I fought back blushing.

"You're different," he laughed.

"I feel the same about you," I said, then wondered if that matched with what he meant.

Benedict winced as the group around us ooh and aahed. Dragon217 pulled me into a game of *Street Fighter* and Elana leaned her head against Ferris, who I assumed she was dating. As I traded blows with Dragon217, I felt Benedict's presence out of my view. He was chatting with friends and playing around on an MPC someone had set up. I wanted to talk to him more but I thought there was a pretty good chance I was showing them all how overtly excited and starved for company I really was. I tried to act laidback and failed by thinking I'd forgotten my car keys while the group came to my rescue. Ferris and Dragon217 found them, at the bottom of my own stupid bag, at the same time. I blushed, though, I was secretly touched they cared.

At some point, while I was halfway through kicking Dragon217 in the jaw on *Street Fighter*, he placed a hand on my shoulder. "Hey, Adri-chan. Can we call you that?" I had never received a nickname before. "Sure!"

"You can relax here." He gestured around to the group. "We've got your back here."

I couldn't help myself. I jumped up and hugged him and he fell back. Then so everybody could get the same amount of love I started hugging everyone who were just laughing with me until I got to Benedict and I fist bumped him instead. He crinkled an eye and I ran back over to play *Street Fighter*. As Dragon217 positively owned me, I thought about how, after a long period of loneliness, I finally felt a snatch of joy.

That night, I couldn't sleep. My parents snored in the room on the other side of the green-washed wall and I tossed about thinking about Benedict and my new friends. I couldn't wait to see them again. I had finally found My People. My Afro Otaku.

After a few more hours of unsuccessful sleep, I threw off my thin sheet and ran over to my Dell. I looked up my new friends on MySpace and I checked out their pages. Everything about them seemed exciting and cool; they wore various clothes from cons they visited and they listened to indie hip-hop like me. I paused at the pictures of Benedict on his site. He didn't dress up for cons. He stood taller than the group in pictures and threw up a peace sign. While I clicked, I saw Benedict (BPLive) online on AOL messenger along with Ferris (Fargone12), Elana (PixieGirlGirl) and Godai (Dragon217). I was nervous to chat with them but felt much bolder online so I started a group chat in IM with these new friends.

MidnightWanderer477: Hi hi! It's me. Saw you guys up? Playing anything?

Dragon217: MW! Adri-chan.

PixieGirlGirl: My new friend!

Fargone12: hello

BPLive: Hey. Miss you already. Enjoyed spending time with you!

Dragon217: He liked it WAY TOO MUCH

Fargone12: lol

PixieGirlGirl: He's funny.

BPLive: I'm reading light novels right now.

Dragon217: I hate light novels.

MidnightWanderer477: WHOA! So cool!!! Which ones?

BPLive: Just a sec

Then Benedict IM-ed me privately.

BPLive: Hey.

MidnightWanderer477: Hi!!

BPLive: It's easier to talk this way without everyone around. It's easier to talk to you honestly this way. I can be kind of shy in person. Not my best attribute. I'm sorry if I didn't say too much today.

MidnightWanderer477: You were great! I'm the same way!! I totally understand. It sucks. I actually have social anxiety but I'm trying to take acting classes to get better at being in public.

BPLive: How's that going? I'd like to see you in a play.

MidnightWanderer477: Really??! I'd be so nervous. But I'd love if you come!! I can't wait to go to your DDR competition.

BPLive: I'm nervous too but I'd definitely be happy if you came.

MidnightWanderer477: I will!!! Do you like to dance in clubs and things? Since you're so into DDR?

BPLive: It's not the same type of dancing. I actually hate that kind of dancing.

MidnightWanderer477: Oh. OK

BPLive: Oh no! If you like it, that's fine!

MidnightWanderer477: I've never been to a club! But I like to dance in my room a lot.

BPLive: Haha, me too. It's embarrassing.

MdinightWanderer477: No way!

BPLive: I can't wait to see you again. I probably should go to bed. I really can't wait.

MidnightWanderer477: Me too!!!! Sleep well, BPLive!

BPLive: You too, Adri-chan.

That night I jumped into bed and wriggled around, near delirious with happiness. I finally had friends, folks who would talk to me when I was lonely at night. Plus, I'd found the first guy I wanted as a boyfriend. Not only had I found a guy I genuinely, quickly, already liked, I'd found a kindred spirit, someone who was a relief and thrill to chat with about mutual interests. I didn't know what to expect at the competition but I dreamed of Benedict, sleeping next to me in the open space. I didn't imagine us really having sex or doing anything interesting, I didn't even know what we'd do, I just imagined myself hugging his long body, back first, like it was my personal pillow and I fell asleep happily. I wondered if he was thinking about me too.

The day of the competition I messaged Elana and Dragon217, who often dressed up for these things, and asked them what to wear. Elana still had her twists in but she planned to pin them up in two full moon-shaped buns like Usagi and have on a simple black shift. Dragon217 was going to wear hoop earrings and a halter top. Ferris was wearing a gi, since he would be coming out of kendo classes. After consulting them I chose a tutu, a *Samurai Champloo* shirt and vinyl-shaped earrings. I put on bright red lipstick and make-up, which I normally never did. I pinned a stripe of purple into my shoulder-length bob.

We met outside of Anime World. We shivered with excitement and Benedict had on yet another plaid shirt, this one striped red, and extremely baggy jeans. When he saw me he blinked quickly, then looked away. We didn't waste too much time in Anime World and drove as a group up and down in Ferris's van to the Dave & Buster's in Homestead. We listened to Dragon217's CD of Deltron 3030 on the way and sang along to "Mastermind." Benedict was riding shotgun and I was sandwiched between Ferris and Elana, my big tutu spreading on their legs. Dragon217 sat alone in a solitary seat in the back of the van and he was playing a Game Boy.

Benedict, who in my head had been dubbed as the group's leader, usually participated in singles competitions: he liked dancing solo. Dragon217 thought DDR was stupid, but according to Elana he was technically just as good as Benedict but he'd never participated in tourneys. Dragon217 and Benedict traded a few conversations about how best to choose songs and he prepped Benedict mentally. I kept rooting, whipping the group up into a frenzy. By the time we reached the D&B, we were hyped and ready.

The arcade in Homestead was far more populated than The Mills. Teenagers and early college-aged students like us milled about; racked up points on racing games, they played pinball and *Galaga* and threw fiercely at electronic dartboards. There were a group of kids around our age stuck in clusters around the DDR machine, eager and practicing fast steps on the floor. They danced in a way I hadn't seen before, their legs scissored and stepped to the right, flailed out, and then back in. It was definitely a unique experience to watch. They all seemed so good.

When the competition started, I saw how great they all really were. Fuchsia lights flew out of the machine, drenching us in their glow. I could barely catch the competitors' feet as they moved in a flurry and the points on the neon-lined machine rocketed up. The directional arrows flashed pink and blue. I generally didn't dance to these kinds of songs, they were frenetic and wild but still somehow metronomic. While watching some of the dancers I noticed how flawless they were. I glanced over at Benedict to see if he were worried. Benedict's head was bobbing up and down to the beats blasting from the machine, his eyes were black and focused, as if in another world.

When it was his turn, we cried his name and he waved one hand back at us but didn't turn around. He wasn't the same Benedict I knew from Anime World. This Benedict was like the Hitokiri Battosai, mild-mannered and kind in the everyday, but when he was plugged in, he inhabited someone fearsome and committed.

Benedict leapt up on the Konami machine and when the song started his legs flew around so furiously I couldn't see his feet. The crowd went silent at first then ooh and ahhed as the points surged upward, faster than his partner, a thin white boy with a Slipknot shirt and dyed-orange hair. I cheered so hard my mouth hurt. The points kept going up and Benedict easily defeated his opponent. I couldn't believe it. I heard him talk about how much he loved DDR but I had never seen how talented he actually was. Stars surged in my eyes. Benedict went up against several more players, some teenagers, some our age, some in their forties and he beat all of them. He went on to the final round and my heart was pumping wildly, I clutched Dragon217 and he grabbed me happily as we jumped up and down and squealed. Elana ran in circles and Ferris stood with his arms crossed, an eyebrow cocked; his eyes were fixed forward. The rest of the crowd was crying for Benedict too. He didn't look back at any of us; he was on a mission. His last opponent was an orb-bellied, red-bearded kid with a Bloodhound Gang shirt and he was incredible. He and Benedict were neck-in-neck the entire face-off until Benedict pulled forward at the very end and used a knee drop to secure a long arrow on his last move and nailed the win. Our group cried out. I was flabbergasted that this man who'd I recently met, who'd been so kind and introduced me to my first new friends, was incredible at DDR. I couldn't believe my terrific fortune.

When Benedict finally realized he'd won, he snapped out of his trance and saw the points. The other bearded guy gave him a friendly side-hug and he blinked, stunned. He looked quickly to the crowd and saw all of us cheering for him and he looked straight at me and grinned huge. Then he pumped his fist at all of us and we roared. He'd won $1,000 and pledged to treat us all to a big meal at Dave & Buster's in celebration. I wanted to run over and hug him but I was too shivery-minded. He jumped off of the machine, ran to our group and raised a palm to me first. I slapped his hand back.

"That was tough," he said, wiping a sheet of sweat off of his brow. "I can't believe I won."

"You were amazing!" I said and slapped his palm again, wishing I could hug him.

"Thanks, thanks," he said, blushing.

"Yeah, you were all right, man," Ferris said. Elana squealed and jumped on his back. He shook her off, laughing. "Girl, my body is SO sore."

Dragon217 grinned and said, "You've gotten so much better."

Benedict winked. "Told you."

We started to walk out of the arcade to have dinner in the Dave & Buster's, when I felt a fresh shadow. Benedict and the group kept walking, but I noticed the shadow approaching my skirt and I tugged Benedict's rolled up sleeve. "Company." Benedict whipped his head around and the shadow illuminated the face of another similarly tall Black guy who was drunk and red in the face. "I bet on your partner," he spit. "You fucked it up."

"Whatever, man," Benedict said and turned. The shadow materialized into a long-bodied man with a short fade, a goatee and Benedict's eyes.

"Fuck," Benedict said and bent down and whispered in my ear. "That's my brother. He knew about this but he said he wouldn't come. He's trying to fuck me up." Then he said to his brother, "Leave me out of your shit, Eldridge."

I piped up, unnecessarily. "Benedict just won. We're going to celebrate. If you want to come you can, if you don't…"

Eldridge smirked. "Your girl?"

Benedict edged over and moved in front of me. "Adri-chan, let's just go."

"Didn't think you had any game, man," Eldridge said. "But you found your match. A weird ass nerd like you. Is she wearing a *tutu* right now?"

At this, Benedict started forward and I grabbed his arm. "It's cool! I know I'm weird," I said.

Benedict gently removed my hand and said, "Hey. I'll take care of this."

He tried walking a few steps forward and his brother leapt forward too.

"I'm fucking sick of your shit," he said. "You keep getting money doing this weird nerd shit but you don't give it to your own brother. Ever."

Benedict replied, "The money is going to Pops. I actually want him to live."

They went back and forth about their dad and I surmised from the conversation that their father, not the best guy, was dying somewhere in the Caribbean and Benedict was apparently doing all the legwork taking care of him from Pittsburgh. His brother was losing money fast trying to stay afloat after he'd lost his job at Target.

Finally, his brother said, "Let Dad die. He was bad to Mom and never did a thing for me. He's a fucking loser and so are you."

I was getting pissed myself at this point and I opened my mouth to defend Benedict, but in the process his brother laughed and reached forward and grabbed my ass under my tutu and said "It's meh, her ass. Tits are huge though." I shrieked and shoved him off and when he tried again to reach for me again Benedict grabbed him by the collar and threw him into an arcade machine that abruptly collapsed as he fell into it.

"Don't. Don't you dare fuck with her," Benedict said, his curls were spiking up from head and swaying. A halo of light fell around his head and he threw his hands forward. A ball of fire surged between his palms and he wrenched his arms back.

"Benedict, Benedict!" my friends roared.

"Don't do this for me," I said, eyes stretched and bugging out.

Benedict, in full power mode, didn't hear me anymore. His brother rose from the shreds of the racing machine, brushed the dust off of his shoulder and laughed. "That was cute," he said.

His brother cupped his hands and a red flame emerged, sizzling scarlet. He shoved it at Benedict and Benedict easily dodged it. They traded blows of fire, dodging and running and blasting. Sometimes Benedict had the upper hand, sometimes Eldridge did. It wasn't until Benedict found an opening when his brother bent over too slowly that Benedict shot a long stream of light at his stomach and his brother got hit, hard. He was shocked, slumped, fell over, done. He shouted out Benedict's name but Benedict walked away from him.

On the Dave & Buster's floor, his brother writhed and wriggled. Benedict wiped his face and I ran over to him. Back to being the man I cared for so much in so little time, his eyes flashed human and he was warm again. He breathed my name hoarsely. He wrapped one arm around me and his head collapsed onto my shoulder.

"I'm tired, Adri-chan," he said. "What a day."

I stroked his curls and he leaned his huge body on me as I struggled to walk forward. Ferris and Dragon217 caught him and we all eased him back onto an empty restaurant booth.

"I'm okay," he said to me. "Let's eat somewhere else."

Benedict spent most of his winning DDR money on his father's healthcare, but he used the remaining funds, which weren't much, to take us all out to breakfast at midnight at an Eat N' Park nearby. We—Ferris, Dragon217, and Elana and I—all huddled together in a blue booth and ate thin pancakes and talked about anime. We weren't thinking about loneliness, fathers, brothers, family, or new environs.

Benedict leaned his head on the window while we were talking and stared out. He looked black-eyed. I worried about him. I scanned my new friends with love, these Afro Otaku. I glanced at Benedict and knew that I loved him too, in my special way.

"Hey," I said to him.

He peeked up at me from the window. "Adri-chan." "Thank you for saving me," I said.

He waved a hand. "I didn't save you. You don't need saving. I just got pissed off. I'm sincerely sorry." "Not talking about Dave & Buster's," I said gently. He stared at me long and reached a hand over, grasped mine. I felt his quick warmth, clutched his back.

The Afro Otaku saw us clutching hands and Elana reached over and took my free fingers. Ferris took hers. Dragon217 took his. We clutched hands, hard. There we were, just a funny little group of the strangest of Pittsburgh people.

3

For August Wilson and Romare Bearden

I *was born to a time of fire.*
The piano hollers a pastiche of past, in singing colors, cut clean as quilt block. The sound sizzles, leaps and roars. Wilson's old piano is chattering about spirits, the sweet songs of the enslaved and secret lore. Maybe love. I can't tell what the folks at the front of this jazz joint are swooning about, because I'm focused on how they are playing wild.

We are in Pittsburgh, atop August's Hill.

Black bodies encircle me as my friends and I huddle in clusters, listening, listening.

A sax screams, drumskin aches and writhes, neon violet surges from the deep cave of trumpets and splashes us all in the crowd, drenching us in its glow. We want to clap but we're stunned by the sound.

Everybody got stones in their passway. You got to step over them or walk around them. You picking them up and carrying them with you.

The piano keys shudder, holler. The lights in the scarlet place redden deeper. The floorboards warm up with yellow, scorching our feet.

We can hear Wilson's voices as we've always heard them, in the thrum of our roiling lines, in the Black of our fingers, in the smile of our sisters.

"What's the point of *The Piano Lesson*?" asks my friend Benedict, who sits beside me. He watches the band play, his eyes purpl'd and transfixed. He read the play many times and saw his mother's face in Wilson's stories. "That ghosts haunt you but you're the only one who can release them?"

"Is a ghost always a spirit? Is a spirit always a ghost?" I say back, thinking of my grandfathers and father and mother and the children I might or might not have or the legacy that I still have not begun to think about because I am too old and too young at the same time. Still chasing Wilson and Bearden's coattails.

"I don't know," Benedict says.

All you got to do is set them down by the side of the road. You ain't got to carry them with you.

We are young and know little about True Lessons or satisfying conclusions. We say nothing then and let the jazz carry our burgeoning loads, our youth-sweetened tears, our generational pains and that which we must pass down.

4

The Text Message

I didn't have a cell phone, and had pretty much no one to text until I was a sophomore in college. The first text message I ever received was from Benedict Duncan, a young man I had a massive crush on. He was a fellow Afro Otaku, one of our group of anime nerds. I was in my room, prepping for Psych 100 and trying to decipher my terrible scribble-scratch notes on Professor Heron's lecture. My life had just started to pick up. I was small-bodied and strange, and I had just met my first new friends, a mixed group of anime nerds like me at an abandoned mall during the summer and was still so proud to know them. They compelled me to make major changes in my life. I moved out of my parents' house and found a roommate, an Indonesian girl named Lady. She lived with me in the dorms at Pitt and taught me how to smile and say terimah kasih with some flair. I still didn't have a car, but I learned the bus line and journeyed all over Pittsburgh, gobbling up the exciting bodies and electric conversations around me.

Benedict, who I had dubbed the Afro Otaku leader, had taken my new friend group on many excursions I couldn't access on the bus. We went to the Waterfront to see *Twilight* when it first came out, we waded in the rippled, dark face of Lake Erie waters after we caught RED in concert, we saw jazz shows on the Hill, we drove up to Cleveland to see a showing of *Death Note* in an indie theater. These were joyous times and Benedict had shown me great kindness, though I didn't want us to simply be good friends. Every time we got close, something stopped us, an invisible wall, or the constant, immediate eyes of friends. At movies, our arms pressed close, he always ruffled my curls and I always poked him in the back. I couldn't tell how he felt about me, but I'd never had a boyfriend before, being a massive dork in school, and I dreamed that Benedict would be the first one.

My glistening Nokia flip phone buzzed off my armoire and I caught it with one hand. I snapped it open and on the screen I saw a simple "Hey."

I stared at it and recognized the phone number as Benedict's. I could feel my pulse in my fingertips. I immediately called him and said, "Hey," as chill as possible, although calling him that fast wasn't very chill.

"Adrienne! I texted you. You're supposed to text back," he laughed.

"I assumed you just wanted to talk," I said. "I have to press a lot of buttons just to say hi back and what if you had something important to say?"

"Okay. Anyway, I was wondering if you're free and want to see me, just for a bit?"

"Of course. I always want to see you." I wanted to bite back the last sentence, seem coy, but I liked him so much I didn't care how I looked.

"Awesome. I'm just walking around in a circle at Squaw Run Park since I just got off. You're close right? Can you meet me there?"
"Sure!"

"Great."

"You were planning to text all of this?" I asked.

"I just believed in myself."

We hung up the phone and I fell on my back on my chartreuse comforter. I shut my eyes, opened them. I stared at my small legs. He didn't properly ask me out on a date. He just wanted me to come to a park in the winter? Why? He usually was earnest and transparent, rarely mysterious, but I suppose there were more things to learn about him. His voice also sounded a little darker than usual, tinged with something blue I had yet to uncover.

The day was typical for Pittsburgh in November, the temperature was dropping rapidly, the city preparing for a long, shaggy freeze. Thick, dead clouds grayed the city. Squaw Run was flanked by shivering trees that wagged and stilled in the cool wind; a lake sat in the center of the park. I kicked away dark slush bunched in patches on the grass and looked up to see Benedict on the other side of the lake. He wore a black peacoat, fog slipping from his lips. He strode forward slowly, distracted, and the very few people in the park were occupied with strolling along or chatting on benches. I called out to him on the other side of the lake and he stopped, glanced up, hearing me immediately. When he saw me, he beamed.

I ran, a little too quickly, over stray ice, to catch up with him on the other side. When I reached him he grabbed both of my elbows, "Whoa whoa, don't slip." I grabbed his arm back and felt his soft-strong bicep through his coat.

We broke and he looked down at me, his eyes narrow with visible pain.

"Benedict?"

"Yeah," he said. I wanted to reach up and lay my hand on the bulge of his cheekbone. I tried to restrain myself but did it anyway, sweetly. His looked a little startled but didn't remove my hand. Trying to cover it up I said,

"If we stay out like this you're going to get a fever," I said. "Let's go inside."

His eyes softened. "Okay. I don't want you to get cold."

"Let's go somewhere. Get something to eat."

"No. I need to do this now."

I took a step back, surprised. This Benedict wasn't my Benedict in that moment. He was inaccessible, insistent.

"I'm leaving tonight," he went on. "I'm going to Honduras. That's apparently where my father is from. Was from. He never knew, but now that he's dead I have to be with his people, and they are all apparently in Honduras. I have to take him back to his family. I don't know how long I'll be gone but I wanted to tell you in person and without the group around all the time."

The ice in the air pressed against me and suddenly felt so cold I could cry. He was leaving. Going. My first crush. After I'd just met him. And he was in unfathomable pain right now and I couldn't do a thing for him.

He saw the look on my face and said quietly, "I'm sorry."

"What in the world would you be sorry for?" I said, blinking, trying to make my expression look more even. "*I'm* so, so sorry. For you. And your family."

"Thank you, Adri," he said. He reached forward with one long arm and swept me into a hug. I hugged him back, hard. The fabric from his coat itched my nose and I didn't care. He sat his chin atop my head.

"It sucks. It does. It all sucks."

I leaned my head against his chest. I wondered what a couple--were we even that--would do in a K-Drama. Try again anyway? Would I go with him? What would I do? Tears pricked my eyes for many reasons and Benedict breathed out and released me.

"All right."

We never dated but it felt like a hard break.

"I'm in love with you," I spit out thinking Tsukushi from *Hana Yori Dango* might say something that. Speak some kind of romanticized truth when the world was revolting against us. As I said it, I regretted it.

I'd never seen someone's mouth fall open in real life, but his did just then. He kept staring at me, blinking. I turned in the opposite direction prepared to run off for a little bit, realizing I'd just humiliated myself and ruined a friendship with one of the only people I really liked.

He saw me positioned to leave and he reached out a hand. "Hey, Adri-chan, hey. Please don't go. Sorry. This is a lot of information to process right now."

"No, that was sudden, it was ridiculous," I said. "Bad timing. I'm here for you regardless."

"Look, I'm in love with you too," he said but it came out as a sigh. It was my turn for my eyes to bug out.

"Really?"

"Of course. I thought it was pretty obvious." He smiled. "I just don't know what I can do about it right now. There's just too much going on. I wanted to tell you the same thing, I just thought it would be selfish. But here we are."

"You're probably one of the least selfish people I've ever met," I said.

"You think these great things about me, but I'm really just some guy who didn't even know his dad was from Honduras until yesterday. I don't know any Spanish. I don't know what the hell I'm going to do when I get there."

"What do you want to know in Spanish?" I asked. "My mom is Puerto Rican. I can probably figure it out."

He kicked a bit of slush away from his leather shoe and looked at me in a way he hadn't before. He was hungry, eager, tenderly masculine.

"How do you say 'I love you' in Spanish?" he said, then he moved his head closer to mine and said it in a breath. "Te quiero?"

I swallowed and nodded. I said, "Te adoro. Te amo. Te quiero too."

"All of those," he said. Looming over me, he leaned down, brushed my curls from my mouth and kissed me long, gently, sweetly. I kissed him back just as softly and he separated from me. My face was scarlet, his eyes darted over my face.

"I don't know when I'm coming back to Pittsburgh," he said. "If I'm coming back anymore. He was my only family outside of my brother. This sucks so bad."

"I'll wait for you," I said, as if it were obvious. There was still a chance. I could be there for him. I didn't want him to be alone.

"No way," he breathed out. "No. I want you to have a fun college life not waiting on me. Especially since you were out there at Fox Chapel High and we were your first friends. I just want you to have a good life. Isn't that what love dictates?"

I didn't know what else to say. He'd made his decision. It was all so frustrating. I reached out and hugged him and he embraced me back tightly.

"If you come back, you better find me," I said.

"Deal," he said. We clutched each other as the Pittsburgh cold bit our brown faces. I loved his giant body and I was terrified to lose him, but here I was. Losing someone I cared for so easily. I'd lost my cousin, my best friend outside of my sister, in a car accident and my dad to a lifelong alcohol addiction, but I'd never lost a boyfriend before. We stood in front of the lake, the loss heavy and engulfing. Still, we were in love, even for that little bit of time.

Benedict went back the next day, and my life returned to normal, jaggedly. It felt hollow without Benedict, and the Afro Otaku group at the Pittsburgh Mills gradually broke up as Ferris, the Afro'd kid who did kendo, graduated and Dragon217 transferred over to CMU and started hanging out with a new crew. Elana and I remained friends and we traded funny videos online but things weren't the same. My roommate Lady and I became close as I drifted away from the Afro Otaku. I still hadn't figured out my phone.

A few months later, I received a text. It simply said, "Hey," and without even seeing the number I knew who it was. This time I didn't call him back.

"Hey," I wrote back after 20 minutes, not knowing how to figure how to text. "I miss u."

"I miss u 2," he wrote back. "Should have said it before. Miss u so much. Goodbye."

And after that text I didn't hear from Benedict Duncan for the next two years.

OAV

Neon Steel

She woke up in the alley, bare-fleshed and bold. Humans had this problem; flesh terrified or thrilled or enticed them into trouble whereas Nadia knew the ramifications and beauties of skin. Which is why she chose this medium-sized body, that of a regal-dark woman with purpl'd locs and a scar on her cheek that hadn't healed after a Surgery she didn't remember. In any case, she knew she was a Black woman, fresh-feeling and Caribbean American. She knew she was first to fight, unbending and sweet-minded. She was fiery, difficult to decipher, ghosts wriggling in her head. Under the layer of brown was smooth machinery; coating her body was glistening wire; her secret in the human world, year 1987. The only possible way humans would know her Real Identity is if they caught a glimpse of her hand, wrapped in black glove, hiding the one betrayal this body possessed. The hand was robotic, her true self. But why would strangers pull off something shadowed, a piece of her, in the first place?

The air was typical for a city that most would call cold. Dry, grit-specked and gray, with that deadening Pittsburgh chill. Black sooted and river-streaked. Still she smelled something scarlet, the color of a red petal. She wasn't used to smelling beauty in human alleys, but she realized she was just smelling her own perfumed body. The place around her was adrip with brown liquids from trash heaps, and the cement was rough and mean. She stood up slowly and scanned the alley. She breathed and the place smelled better. It smelled good, like her. A few shadows slammed open a bar door nearby and they stopped, regarded her, glistening and gorgeous.

They approached her because, of course they would. She slid past them and when they got in close, they stopped, a bit confused themselves why they didn't try to pounce on a naked woman. They looked at each other, these drunk shadows, then they looked at her and trembled. Then they passed on. She grabbed one of them as he was leaving. He threw out a hand to touch her and she gripped his fingers with her cold, robotic hand fiercely. She wrenched him back and stole his shirt, it was blue.

She threw it on and it covered her just enough. She would have taken his pants too but they were unattractive and dirt-grimed.

The shadows flew off and she wrenched open the door to the bar, adjusting the glove on her hand.

It was frothing with bubbling voices, as funky as feet. Fast-blinking blue and scorching pink lights draped a cloud of pulsing bodies. She pushed them all aside as she surged through the crowd. Hands reached out to grab her and she shoved them off easily. No time to dance, though this little body loved to dance.

If she could find Dr. Cobbler this would just be done with. The whole thing was easy. Go back to before the War, kill Dr. Cobbler while he was still fucking around in Pittsburgh clubs in his mid-thirties. Smooth and simple. In her world, she fought for justice, this Black Robot girl who wore human skin. She wanted a Good World in the future and that demanded sacrifices in this former time. Therefore, one sacrifice: Dr. Cobbler deserved to die. He'd killed children, mothers, daddies, and programmed Her People, the tech-human hybrids who were constructed to aid humans, to destroy their world until it burned and simmered. She cared for humans and tech and hybrids like her but Dr. Cobbler was different. A killer deserved to be killed. The humans were always debating "an eye for an eye or a tooth for a tooth" or "do unto others as they do unto you" but she preferred to shoot a bullet through that eye or crack that tooth in half.

Speaking of guns, she unfortunately hadn't come with one and in the process of Transportation she'd lost her clothes and good ol Hers, her little violet rifle. So she was bare-handed but that was okay. She'd once taken a guy out during the War with a toothpick so she'd figure it out.

What a strange place for Dr. Cobbler to be, she thought, as she scanned the joint. She saw a space at the bar, frothing with rainbow people, and sat down carefully. Men flew in, talking about fizzing drinks and she punched them off.

"Jesus Christ. Someone had a Walk of Shame," the bartender said. He was tawny, strong-jawed but slinky. He had taut, hardened muscles that looked like they'd been shaped in the human military and smoothed out with day labor. Still, here he was getting humans hammered in here.

She blinked and winced. Human humor was stupid. "I'm just here looking for someone."

"This wouldn't be the first time I saw a girl wander in here in old clothes crying about some guy."

"I don't care about Some Guy. I'm looking for somebody specific."

"You can tell me who. I know how to keep secrets."

"Nope," she said.

He half-smirked and winked, "I'm going to get you some clothes. You want something while you wait?"

"No," she said and turned to look at the crowd again. Big leaping breasts tossed around in red dresses, the drag queens on the floor stomped and stamped with shapely, flailing legs. Glitter was stretched across flashing faces.

The man called another bartender, a small balding guy, to take over and slipped out the back. She wondered why he would have random clothes on the ready in the first place and she decided she wouldn't trust him. But she would take his clothes. Ripe music sounded holy over thumping rhymes as folks nodded, clapped nodded. The crowd rippled as two dark suited men slipped in and a man with a burgundy lapel slipped upstairs to the VIP room with them. She stood up. God, if only it could be this easy. To regain the life she'd lost, to return back home to the warm arms of the only humans she loved, her Mami and Daddy. To fulfill the mission of her only friend Maya, Dr. Cobbler's defected graduate student. Those people had raised her after she escaped from Dr. Cobbler's Tech farm. She only had to take this asshole out.

She surged forward and the bartender tugged her back gently. She turned around, irritated.

"I have something to do."

"Here, just chill the fuck out for a second," he said and gave her a folded-up pair of leggings and a pair of heels.

"Sorry about the heels. They don't look comfortable. You're so lucky my best friend is a queen who plays tonight" he said. "And that this girl is nice. You should say thank you to her."

"Okay. Thanks," she said and grabbed his leggings and heels. She stepped into the leggings, rolled them up to her knees and tried on the heels. They were fun to wear, simple. Why did human women love these so? She preferred bare feet but didn't want a nail to jam through her foot.

"OK, I'm just going to let you do what you do," he said.

She started toward the staircase and he playfully tapped her back.

"You seem stuffy. Seriously. Let me get you something to drink. You look like you need water."

She ignored him. She heard him tell the other bartender he needed a few minutes and she hoped he would leave her alone. It didn't matter anyway. She ran forward, pushing aside folks from the crowd as she slipped through shadowy spaces. Still she felt the bartender on her heels.

"I'm Hylo," he called to her back. "What's your name? You seem like you need a friend." She could put this bitch in a headlock but since he helped her out she'd let him go. Plus, instinctively, he seemed harmless. If she were human, she'd think he was a little bit sexy.

Still, she didn't like having conversations while she was focused on a task. But this guy wouldn't let up. She got to the stairwell and looked up at a red rope barring her from the second level. There were only two guys guarding Dr. Cobbler. This should be fine. Hylo lingered nearby then loomed over her. He was really irritating at this point and needed to get out of the way.

"Please go back to your job, Hylo," she said and swung around in his direction. She bared her teeth and flapped him away.

"No," he said firmly and leaned over and smiled. "Because you're up to something. And this is *my* bar."

"That's sweet of you to protect it," she said, and threw one gloved hand around his neck. "But you're out. Right now."

He struggled under her grip and his eyes near bugged out. He fell to the ground and she released him.

"Fuck, man." He got to his knees.

Her eyes stretched. Now wasn't the time to give away her secret. While he was recovering she slunk up the stairs and this time he accompanied her brazenly.

"Look, I'm just going to follow you. Dark/Angel Woman. Something-something whatever your name is."

"It's Nadia," she said and dodged a man coming her way. She hated people giving her nicknames. She got to the end of the rope and two men in black shirts that gripped heaving chests barred her from going in.

"She's with me," Hylo said over her head. "She can go through."

One of the men cocked an eyebrow. "Sorry, Hylo. She can't. There's a guest you can't see tonight."

Nadia rolled her eyes. She noticed the gun on his holster and relief washed over her swiftly. At least she didn't have to strangle Dr. Cobbler with his own tie or something. While the man was talking to Hylo, she quickly got his gun from below the belt. She pointed it at him. Hylo kicked the other man in the stomach and grabbed his gun. Then, the two men leapt toward them. Hylo kicked his guy down the stairs and Nadia kneed her guy in the balls then also shoved him down the stairs. This, of course started a commotion in the club below but Nadia's eyes were locked on Hylo and his were locked on hers. They both drew together, at roughly the same time, and stared each other down.

"OK. Looks like you aren't the most trustworthy person," she said and winked. "Thanks for the pants."

"Never said I was trustworthy," he laughed and shook his gun. "Put yours down."

"You're protecting Dr. Cobbler, which means you have to go too. Sorry. You seemed like you might be nice."

"You're not a criminal, Nadia," he said. "But sorry, yeah. I'm gonna protect my bar."

There was a rustle of noise and a few women in v-cut dresses screeched and ran from the VIP after seeing Nadia and Hylo with their guns drawn. A man emerged from the back, he was shivering and white-suited and confused.

"What the fuck is going on here?" he said. He held his hands up.

Nadia immediately recognized him. She started to move away from Hylo to shoot Dr. Cobbler in his bulgy temple. Hylo kept one eye on her and cocked his gun. She prepared to take him out him, too, but he swung his arm around and shot a bullet through Dr. Cobbler's head.

He threw the gun on the floor, kicked it to her and raised his hands in surrender. Nadia fell back, stunned. Her gun was still drawn and fury and relief and chilly fear washed her clean. She looked back at Hylo and with her free hand carefully picked up his gun too and pointed both at him. Still. Still. Still.

"You stole that from me. That was big," she spit, keeping her voice a steady line.

"I told you you're not a criminal," he said, then softly, "Nadia."

"You don't know me," she said, but lowered her gun. She didn't know why she lowered it.

Because he did know her, didn't he? She didn't know how, but he somehow knew her. He walked toward her slowly, as if she were a bomb ready to detonate, as if he were gauging her reaction. He gestured toward her gloved hand.

"I know what's under the glove. TH1-MONICA. That's your real name. I gave you that name when I was working on you with Dr. Cobbler. Now you're Nadia."

His name in her mouth sounded like violet petals swinging.

He kept coming forward. "You loved me. A real long time ago. You lost your memories in the War but I knew I'd find you in some iteration of time. It took me awhile, waiting for you, getting this job, figuring out when you'd arrive, but I knew you'd come to this one. If not for me, for revenge."

He reached out a hand and she took a step back.

"I'm my own daughter," she said but her voice sounded soft. She looked at his face and remembered the scent of his smile. Cigarettes and cherry blossoms. Why? When had she been so close? What about love? Wasn't it just fine to love? Couldn't she be her own woman and still love?

"Of course you are," he said. "But come on. Remember me too."

He reached over, softly swept a loc from her face and pressed the side of her temple sharply.

She remembered him too then. The lithe dark-browed soldier-scientist who watched Dr. Cobbler make hybrids of tech and humans at MIT. Dr. Cobbler was the originator of her kind of Tech in the first place. Hylo had once believed Tech and humans and hybrids could coexist. Still, he was always attached to Dr. Cobbler, his professor, a mirror of him, the one who had created Nadia and the other Tech. Hylo risked everything to leave Dr. Cobbler after the doctor sold his Tech to the American government, and Hylo was always on the run. But Hylo wasn't like Dr. Cobbler, was he? He was fair and kind-minded, not angry. Still, his pseudo-father tried to destroy hybrids and humans and Tech all together, by reprogramming all of the Tech he'd created to kill humans. Humans of course saw Tech as the enemy and they fought back, resulting in the War. Hybrids were also on the chopping block even though they were both human and Tech. Dr. Cobbler, apparently, simply wanted to Watch the World Blaze before he burned it all down, as men like him always did. And so he burned it.

Her family went first, killed by humans who hated both Tech and hybrids. And she escaped, helped by a woman called Northern who guided her across sleek rivers, following moonlight, where she was so tired she lost her longings and slake.

Dr. Cobbler's reprogramming hadn't worked on her, and she never knew why. After many years of running on her own, she met up with Hylo in a short bar on Broadway in Nashville. He was a bartender there too. She didn't remember him back then either. They kept finding themselves, again and again, in different cities. Back then he'd erased her memories too and without them she went running.

The hard part was when Hylo and Nadia fell in love. A secret kiss under a sloped, fresh-bloomed Sakura tree. She was sitting on the bench, reading and he came over and said roughly, "When you're done reading, get up and kiss me." So she finished a few pages then got up and kissed him. Then, there was a cuddle on a Massachusetts baycliff. She'd catch helicopter seeds in her hands and watch them fall and he said something about how the cloven things were always spinning, like her. There were hard times too. When he'd saved her from exploding houses and cherry bombs from the humans, other times she'd saved him from human snipers and Tech rifles. She showed him how to ride a motorcycle and he bought his own, red, and drove it down Hillwood. All of these moments of high and low drama amounted to love and of course when Dr. Cobbler found out about the two, he went after her in Nashville too.

Hylo helped her escape back then, and she watched him disappear, in a swift explosion of the bar meant for both of them, never to return. She was saved by Maya Dream, the graduate assistant, who had created a time portal a long while back. She also had erased Nadia's memories of Hylo, given her the mission simply to *Kill Dr. Cobbler, Save Us All* so the robot-girl went back in time to stop the destruction. She remembered Maya and Dr. Cobbler, but never Hylo nor the supposed death of him. She knew she had a family who she must avenge, but she could never remember their faces.

Yet, she had forgotten about what had happened in the past, it was old and worn and gone. Why hadn't she remembered? Hylo was still here.

It wasn't just because he and Maya had reprogrammed her to forget about horror or trauma or the human family who raised her. They wanted her to live purely. She had forgotten everything, but still she hadn't forgotten those traumatic parts. All she knew was that she needed Dr. Cobbler to die. Why had she forgotten all of Hylo's love? Why had he reprogrammed her to forget both the good and the horrible? She wanted to at least have That Good. Even if she had to have the horrible too.

Here he was before her. Grizzled as much as he could be with scattered scruff, his skin was always brown and sweet and soft. Here he was alive. Her eyes wet quickly and he shook his head.

"You're not a crier in this iteration of time. I noticed that immediately. You used to cry all the time back when I met you. You're a robot but such a fucking feeler," he laughed. She opened her mouth to say something else but the Men without Guns had returned.

They were red-faced, eyes smoking. One of them lunged after Hylo and he wrestled him down. She used the Big Guy's momentum against him to flip the other guy down and she gave him a solitary kick in the balls too. "Let's get the fuck out of here," he said. "Venga conmigo si tu quiere…"

She punched a guy away from Hylo and he yanked her away from an incoming kick from another bouncer. Barely getting away, they bounded down the stairs and fell out of the bar.

"So what do we do now that we're trapped here in the past?" she said.

He grabbed his keys, jangled them. "My apartment's open tonight. You can meet me there. I'm going to have to go deal with this shit inside. Looks like we fixed the future though."

"You still have that old motorcycle? The Wild One?"

"Of course. Parked out back." He tossed her the keys and she caught them.

Outside, she approached the corner of the sidewalk and saw it immediately. Purpl'd like her locs, he'd painted it from his signature scarlet. The huge, lighted city air cut against her skin, she usually couldn't feel human things like wind but today she felt it, a breath of sharp ice as cold as her hand. She got on the bike, ripped off her glove, exposing hard wire and silver. She started the engine, felt the wild rush of bike, the steel-cold night and the possibility of snow. She flew off, into the glorious black city, alone or perhaps not.

5

Viper/Sweet

Fidelicia had about two minutes left before she could blow. For this crowd, she needed to get them shaking and stomping and not snoozing in the back staring at their iPhone-something-something awkwardly like they did at Mr. Smalls when she first started this damn thing. It was the first time she was the headliner and, bitch, she had to pop off. It would be the same song she recorded weeks ago, the same single playing on WAMO, the same song that her Daddy was singing at the steel factory while he worked iron. She'd sliced up enough niggas and girls, got up to this point. She was ready.

The first two acts were her friends, Beastie and Killa Rage or "Lil'", a country redbone born in Macon, Georgia. Girls she'd come up with at Schenley, though Killa knew Wiz back when he was rapping at Allderdice. These were girls she traded glitter pens with; they'd plait each other's hair and swoon and caw. She wanted those girls next to her before she went on and they killed it, DESTROYED THE

STAGE, like she thought they would. They were basically fucking haloed in dynamism. She also invited this kid called Dredge, a skinny little white boy with a dragging beard, who usually unsettled the audience as he stood there just bobbing back and forth with these crazy fucking eyes and you were like who is this kid in the corner trying to act like he's Something and you find out he's actually legit. So he went on, and Fidelicia felt an increase of palm-sweat all over her hands and fiery fear and she tried to forget that her Daddy was in the audience along with her sister Ursula, who didn't think this rap thing was a good idea to begin with. She put them up in VIP, told the barstaff to treat them as good as they could and she floated by every so often, big chest puffed out, swag in place, showing them she ran this spot. U just kept frowning but Daddy was beaming, beaming, beaming.

Ma? She was out. She didn't know where her Ma was. She had disappeared when Fiddy was seven and came in and out like a haunting. Just walked out into the Wilkinsburg cold, in a long, green sweater dress and no shoes, and kept walking. Fidelicia remembered being in bed wondering why Ma was out there in February, where it got so fucking cold ice mossed your skin and you had to run back inside. Fiddy called out for Daddy to come get her mother who was just standing out there smelling the cold and Daddy woke up, saw his wife out the window and then both Fiddy and Daddy bounded downstairs to try to save her but she stretched up and flew away. Got some new wings and just disappeared. The family thought that Ma was dead after all that flying, but she'd stop back in to say *hey*, ghost the family every few years, and Fiddy and Daddy would try to get her to stay, but then she'd fucking soar again. Always in the cold. Always with naked feet. But anyway. It wasn't time for Fiddy to worry about spirits.

She heard the crowd getting hype and getting a little bit irritated because fucking Dredge went over his time, and a lot of them were there for Dredge, but most of them were for her. She heard her name and she wiped the sweat off her bare thighs, exposed in leather shorts that gripped her wobbling ass. She surged forward. Just like any other night, she told herself. Just like any other time. Girl, you know the shit you've seen, those black days, the days the bullets zipped through the headboards while you were sleeping, how your last love from the Hill got dead over some fucking foolishness.

> *Stepping on their noses like yeah I fluff and stuff em.*
> *Crunch and crush and tough it out yeah I fucking rush em.*

That part was harder but it usually established her power early.

> *See them fuckboys coming and I'm like*
> *God bless you boy achoo*

That. Part. Easier. Funny. Stupid. She pointed the songs in her head at the assholes who had used her along the way. The crowd was clapping, she tried to see the VIP section, catch if her Daddy had come up yet.

> *Sick and shivering in this Pittsburgh freeze,*
> *nigga I'm Black and blue.*
> *You wondering how this little Chiquita-Bori do*
> *No your girl ain't never gonna be your goody two*
> *See you saving money to catch me nigga that's on you*
> *Left them boys in their own blood yeah*
> *Nigga I'm one of few*

She saw her friends in the front row and they were egging her on. Light flew up to her face and she felt afire. Daddy and U had made it up to the front and she reached over and

grabbed their hands. The crowd cheered for her. A homecoming, a homecoming.

> *Hollering at the earth so pull them eyes back at me*
> *That sexy-shiny-Miami life with your girl you'll never see*
> *I run this joint and it's like all bitches on me*
> *Shudder at the thought that you bit a bit of me*
> *Ate you up and got back on the bus at Negley*
> *My niggas from the hood nigga you North Allegheny*

The folks pointed at her, she pointed at them.

> *You coming to my house and want to fuck me up allegedly*
> *I know my niggas from the Midwest always got me*
> *I told you before, I'm bright teethed and wilin',*
> *   yeah I'm pretty/ugly*

She scanned the crowd and despite the gusto in the lyrics she
didn't see any of those bitches from North Allegheny or anyone
who wanted to catch her hands. She saw, instead, wriggling,
dancing, loving bodies, heavy with music, the manic crack and
shiver of big backs, the bucking of shivery knees, the fun in
every flailing face. She glowed then, and Daddy came up
and sang along the last lines with her

> *I cut and kill em*
> *Man I'm pretty/ugly*
> *Yeah I cut and kill em*
> *Yeah I'm viper/sweet*
> *I cut and kill 'em*
> *Yeah I'm viper/sweet*

She was about to launch into the last verse when she
sniffed a spirit and she knew who it was. The door creaked

open and the spirit with bare feet floated into a little corner next to the bar, frothing and funky with booze-warm people.

She felt her voice crack and her girl Killa Rage, seeing the spirit from behind the stage, burst forth and saved her, finishing the verse. Then it was her and Killa, whose massive free breasts flopped around, nipples barely smothered with pasties. Beastie, with her passion twists and patchwork skirt (she was weird, not like them really but they kept her around) threw on her purple hat and joined them. They all rapped the lyrics together, and Fidelicia hoped the sound of these loving women would drown out the blare of the red-hot eyes from the Spirt. The spirit whisked the crowd aside like she was flushing open the Red Sea and the folks who knew both Fiddy and the Spirit stepped aside.

Fidelicia reached forward and touched the Spirit's hand and she looked into the face of her mother, which reminded her of her own face.

She finished her bar, *Yeah, I'm viper/sweet*, and she hit the lyrics fiercely, owning that viper in her mouth and she threw it right back at the Spirit. Threw it back sweet. The spirit grasped her hand harder and harder and Fidelicia wrenched hers back and waltzed off, still singing. She had a choice then, like she had for so many years dealing with that old spirit. She could run backstage, cry, fall apart. Or she could fucking destroy the rest of the song, bring joy to these smiling mouths.

Man, I'm viper/sweet

She screamed,

Yeah I cut and kill 'em

The Spirit disappeared again, Fidelicia's music an exorcism.

When the song was over the bodies were clutching bodies ,and Daddy was clapping hella proud and U was pumping her fists and Fidelicia realized she'd created something strange and beautiful with her little song, these lyrics that were supposed to rip open skin like bullets, be all about lady bravado, had instead come and loved everyone, softened them to each other; these folks felt warm and happy and alive just being out and about and laughing and singing. She'd done something Probably Good, she thought.

She finished the set with her girls and jumped off, not thinking about spirits or battles or the crowd anymore. Really, she was the only one left to beat. And they were all cheering her on.

6

Smoke Break

I left Lady for good then got off the bus. It felt right, leaving Lady Prananda. Plus, I thought no way sadness is not not going to happen to this girl right here so I dropped her for good, my supposed best friend, paid one dollar and fifty cents and jumped off at fucking Freeport.

I didn't think about her when I got off at the stop and I didn't look back to see if her nose was pushed hard against the glass, if she were looking for me. I passed the bus stop sign, and the air felt ice-hot, if you know what I'm saying, just spikes of temp-switching stinging that slice thinly through you, and that slicing feeling spreads over your skin and you feel nasty and you're like ugh. The fucking 'Burgh, man. Anyway.

I just went straight over through those cold doors to Giant Eagle, raised my hand to say hey to Damon, the manager, and I went back to the office next to pharmacy and started writing my stupid little puns for the Market District news-letter, which was properly my job. Punny right? (Hands off! This *nacho* cheese.)

She was a douchebag. She was, right? I didn't know. Maybe? I couldn't tell anymore. I really couldn't tell.

She was this short little Indonesian girl (shorter than me!) who delivered newspapers every day at 4am to pay for grad school at Point Park, and she had this really beautiful hair that she could do herself and not go to the salon every week like me. It fell over the front part of her face like a wave of black ocean and, oh fuck it, never mind; the bigger point is that she was just playing mind games with me after her parents found out I wasn't Indonesian. Because APPAR-ENTLY, she LIED and told them my parents were from Jakarta when they were actually Black people from Pitts-burgh, just like me. We were yinzers through and through. *Sorry, Adrienne*, she told them. *I just wanted them to think I wasn't in this country without my people. And they have their ways about Black girls.*

At this point I should have just given up on her but she was my friend, you know? Tight pal. Hip-to-hip. I braided her hair, she styled mine, we went to concerts at Mr. Smalls and saw Viper/Sweet together. She was my best friend. So, I let that shit go.

Then we moved into this three-story place in Oakland together with this stoner named Jake Yee. I was just sand-wiched between these two people from different countries than mine, who were heavy weed smokers, and I had never had sex or done anything cool in my life outside of that time I caped for Mr. Copper after he got busted with all those edibles on campus. Anyway, Jake cooked up zong zi so fine it'd make your damn mouth (down to the teeth!) water so I was cool with him.

Back to leaving her, though. I definitely started trying to imagine a bunch of nasty puns I could shoot at Lady.

Lady: Do you think I'm pretty?

Me: Of course. Pretty ugly.

Or maybe something else. Something more cutting. She had been my fucking BEST FRIEND. And now, and now. No longer punny.

So, here's what led to the drop off. We're in the back of the bus chatting about something useless and then she's on the phone with her dad and he's trying to get her to come back to Jakarta and she's like "Hell no, I'm staying here, with ADRIENNE", and then he just says something in Indonesian that is so loud I can hear it and then she hangs up the phone. I ask her what he said, why she's so mad and she said, "it's not a good word," and I say "what's the word, Lady," and I kind of already know and she says, "it's a bad Indonesian word for…" So I just say forget about it, Lady and I get up and she's like I was defending you, I want to be your friend and I'm just done with all this shit with her so I just start walking to the front of the bus and I just get off. It's all so stupid.

I could feel her in the office as I work, her spirit encircling me as I write. I don't know how to love her right, this friend I've known for so long who so easily dressed me up in a different skin, but she still loved me, right? I didn't know. It was all so tiresome.

When I got back home to our place in Oakland, her bike, a lavender Huffy, was gone. I felt its shadow in her absence and I also wondered why the fuck she was riding it in 10-degree weather after a good bit of snow, and I worried for her. I imagined her, salted in some kind of snow pillar like Lot's wife, somewhere near Centre Avenue; she wouldn't know where the hell she was going. I could imagine that forest-colored winter jacket, too big for her, falling off her frame as she flew. I walked past a chair that had been set out to save a parking spot and right on the porch, smoking weed was Jake Yee, looking high as hell.

"Yo," he said, red-eyed.

"I'm moving," I said immediately. "Done with this shit with Lady."

"She yellow-washing you again?"

"I'm really tired of it. She needs to stand up for herself and own our friendship. Now her parents are dropping the Indonesian n-word and she's gonna probably roll with it."

"Just let it go."

"I'm not going to let it go."

"Let's just fucking smoke, preacher girl. Let's stop thinking about anything complicated tonight."

"I'm so damn tired."

"I know."

Jake Yee led me by the hand and we were inside of his long apartment on the first floor. It was always comforting, the ground adorned with violent-red plush rugs and paintings of Sun-Ra and Marley. The place smelled of crushed paper, Lysol-clean floors and hot kush. He, like Lady, worked at the newspaper; they were MBA grad students who had been on work visas that had expired so they were delivering *Gazettes* off the grid until they could get their documents approved. I was the only one on the lease and they both paid me cash. They had befriended each other, finding out they shared the same situation. I, Lady's friend, just moved in with both. But we were all together.

Jake rolled up his sweater to scratch his elbow, revealing a sleeve of Toots and the Maytals. He waved me over to the table and he started chopping leeks for his fried dumplings. I took over the leek cutting while he rolled out the dough.

"You ladies can fix this."

"No," I said, getting pissed off. I cut the leek as hard as I could. "We plainly can't. Sometimes it's good to just cut certain people out of your life. Abracadabra, badaboom. What do you call a dog magician? A labracadabror!"

"How the hell are you going to cut her out of your life? You can't afford to live in this place without her, and I'm definitely not going to let that one go because I can't afford to live here myself. Oakland is ridiculous now because of the students."

"Okay, then I'll move out," I said.

Jake Yee rolled his eyes and said gently, "Then I'd miss you. And that would be bad for me."

I was almost caught off guard by the hint of softness in his voice but I ignored it. "I think I'm going to move." I was done with the leeks. He had finished rolling the dumplings.

"'Mmkay. In protest I'm not going to help you with not one box. You're on your own, sister."

He said some other shit but I just ignored it. We went over his table and started plopping dumplings in our mouths. He started to light a joint while I ate.

"Anyway, I have an idea."

"Yeah?" I said, preoccupied with the savory meat in the dumpling.

"What if you and me just pretend-date to piss Lady off? You know she likes me."

I sniffed. "Boy, she does not like you."

"Maybe she does. I think she might. It will piss her off."

"Isn't this the plot to some C-Drama we watched last week?"

"Probably," he said. "But it'll be fun. Come on."

"Let me guess," I said reaching over to take a hit. "The first step is to sleep with you. That's not happening."

Jake Yee winked. "Hey, not against it. My family so deeply doesn't give a shit about me in general, so you don't have to worry about Afro-Asian relationship tensions or whatever they fucking call them with me. So, what were you saying about sleeping with me?"

"That I'm not doing it."

"Welp."

"So much for your plan." I handed him the joint back.

"No, I'm serious," he said, leaning forward. "About pretend-dating. I think it would get you the results you're looking for."

I smacked my lips. "Okay."

"Really, girl?"

"Sure," I said, leaning back and heaving air from my nose. "Whatever."

He laughed and took a hit. "Let's make it fun then."

Me and my pal Stills used to hang out in East Lib and get the best, girl, I mean THE BEST, BBQ in the city outside of another Giant Eagle (I'm talking about the one that used to be on Shakespeare Street before the gentrifiers came in and fucked up East Liberty. Gosh, white people.) This dude named Alexander would be just sitting outside on his scarlet Jeep clunker handing out spare ribs and mac and cheese to whomever wanted that shit. And it was always me. He also gave out these 99 cents bootlegged movies and he convinced me to buy *"12 Years of Slavery"* (unintentionally mislabeled). So, Stills and I enjoyed the bad cinematography of this nigga focusing in and out of Fassbender's face while he was sitting in on the movie and licking the BBQ off those sturdy Pittsburgh ribbones.

Stills was a pretty-faced, hulking Nigerian dude, and I'm talking like 7 feet and he talked a lot to me, like way too much but we never hooked up because he reminded me too much of my dad in the face. When he realized I wasn't interested he started just chilling with me as a friend and we'd hang out in my apartment and talk shit and Jake Yee and Lady would join in and we'd have an old time. But after Jake Yee and I decided to fake date, the first person I told to keep this shit on the low was Stills.

I stopped by his apartment, which was down the street from where Lady, Jake Yee, and I lived. I used his spare key, got into the shadowed place, found him on his futon. He was halfway in bed, nose pressed to pillow. I kicked him in the shin and said,

"Yo, Stills. I need to tell you something."

He grumbled and reached for another pillow and pressed it over his head.

"I'm cold. You're loud. Shut up."

"I need you to fake-ify something for me," I said.

"Fake-ify? Girl?"

"Jake Yee and I are going to start dating."

At this he shot straight up. "Fuck. Jake? That skinny Yee. Jesus."

"It's not real. I just want to get back at Lady for constantly hiding her family from me or making up stories about me being Indonesian."

"Ma, WHAT?"

"Listen, I just need you to fake support our relationship, OK?"

He smacked his lips. "God, you're messy. I'm down."

"Okay, great." He reached over and tried to pull me over to him playfully but I shoved him off.

"Sleep well, tiger," I said.

"You're about to get fucked up."

"Of course," I said and shut the door behind me.

Lady finally came home later at night and she went to her room and I just ignored her. I didn't know what to say. At midnight, I'd come to her door and listen to her pant-sleep, and I'd feel guilty for something I didn't even know was bothering me. Then I'd go lie down and I'd hear her get up, come to my room, wait outside. I'd get up, thinking I was going to talk to her, soothe her, but I was done with that shit. So I went back to sleep and I dreamed about rage.

Early in the morning, Lady was gone for work with Jake Yee, and I wondered if Jake Yee would tell her then. They'd already had a shift that started at 4am. I could barely sleep, wondering, wondering. When a creak sounded through the place at 10 in the morning when they were finished, I hoped to see Lady but instead I only saw Jake Yee. He saw me on the third floor peering down and he raised a hand.

"You're not looking for me, I gather?" he said, near haggardly.

"Long shift?"

"Hell. And I have a test on Tuesday. Little American girls don't have to worry about shit like that."

"Try being Black for a day in America."

"Oooh, let's do this another time. Aren't we dating?"

"Lady wasn't with you?"

"No."

"Okay," I said and jumped down the two next flights of steps to see Jake Yee at the bottom. "Yes, we're dating."

He reached into his pocket and produced a cigarette lighter. "Smoke break?" He grabbed our coffees and went outside.

I followed him to the brick porch and we plopped down on the punched-in plastic chairs facing a bleak street with fresh, packed snow. The clouds were low-bellied and grey. Jake Yee shivered in his oversized coat and scanned the street in front of him. I could hear old Steelers reruns seeping from a half-opened window. He raised his skinny legs to his chest and he kept puffing away.

"If we're dating, what's the first thing I need to know about you?"

"I don't know," I said. "That I'm confusing."

"Obviously. Why do you think I thought you'd be down for this?"

"I fell into a trap, then."

"Preacher girls are rarely innocent."

"You're right about that," I said and reached over to take a puff out of his cigarette and coughed on the smoke. He laughed and gently took the cigarette back from me.

"She'll be back in a few. Let's just sit in this horrible cold and reflect on our horrible lives."

"Speak for yourself," I said, pulling my shawl closer to me. "My parents are terrific."

"Who says shit like that? 'My parents are terrific.' No, they fucking aren't. They TRAINED you to say they were terrific to placate you. Your parents are the patriarchy."

"Jesus Christ."

"I like you. That's why we're dating," he said and I realized most of the time I spent with Jake Yee was watching him destroy his lungs and diss his or my parents. I put my legs on the brick rail in front of us and crossed my ankles. I breathed on my coffee to cool it down and watched the empty white road.

"She'll come at any moment," he said. "She was behind me but she seemed really down. I think she really cares about you."

"If she cared about me," I said, sipping on my drink, "She wouldn't let her racist parents get to her."

"So, you're saying that your parents will have ZERO problem with you fake-dating me? They won't be like *oh that girl got yellow fever* or some shit?"

"No. My parents are classy. They love everyone."

"It doesn't mean they don't have their attitudes on the inside. You can lie with your face. I'm sure they do sometimes even though they're 'terrific.'" He drank his coffee.

"Absolutely. But. It's stupid. You don't believe in anyone, do you?"

"No," he laughed and pointed his chin at a couple trying to climb over a snow hump. "I don't."

I slid my eyes at him and winked. "What about your fake girlfriend? Unless we're 'no labels.'"

"I told you I like you," he said, near seriously. I blinked and focused my eyes back on the road. "You're kind of like a guy, Adrienne," he said. "Never letting anyone in. Walls up. All that shit."

"You're fake-dating me, aren't you? Let's just do that."

"Sounds good," he said tartly and puffed on his cigarette.

"Oscar Wilde's last words were: 'this wallpaper goes or so do I.'"

"Are you serious, Adrienne?"

I didn't have time to worry about Jake Yee and his ideas because Lady waltzed by just then with a sex-stained smile on her face. And I mean a Smile. She was fucking beaming and I knew she'd just been with someone in that impossibly short amount of time after her shift and she was staring at her little green phone and it made me so blazingly rabiosa. I felt like my feet were set from toe to top afire. She almost missed the house she was so joyous and I wanted to get up and yank her back on to the road and tell her COME UPSTAIRS. Of course. I was still fucking pissed, it didn't matter how much time has passed. So, she finally realized where we lived and that I was livid and she toddled back up with this little backpack jumping on her shoulders. I wanted to stand up and scream at her but just as I was getting up Jake Yee said "Hey, let's do it now," and I said what? But as I was half-agreeing with him, his face was surging at me and I kissed him back, surprisingly hard, and the shock of it confused me and he kept kissing me back harder and there we were, just fake making out in front of my former best friend. I pushed him off, hot and dry-mouthed, and she was just on the stairs, her mouth hanging open.

I definitely didn't want to even look Jake Yee's way and I pushed my face toward her and just said, "Yeah."

She looked like her face crinkled and fell and I felt horrible but then glorious in my win. She opened her mouth to say something but then she just ran off like a little bitch and I looked over at Jake Yee and his face was red like he was angry at ME. Like ME?

"This was a bad idea," I spit.

"You feel better?" he spit back.

"What the fuck is your problem?"

"You like me too. I felt that pretty clearly. Especially just now."

"I have shit to do right now," I said. "I owe you nothing."

"We're horrible people," he said. "Including Lady. Includ-ing you."

"Give me your cigarette," I grabbed it, tried to smoke and choked.

In my room, alone, I nearly fell asleep when I heard a creaking sound coming from Lady's room. It got louder and louder and then suddenly I heard a low, deep shout rip from the room next to us and I instantly knew it was my friend Stills screwing Lady because he was a stupid idiot too. Jake Yee was right: nobody was to be trusted. I shot up, ran out of my room, and rammed on the door and yelled Lady's name and then she started yelling "Stills!" and riding him harder and I just kicked that door and called her a racist motherfucker until Jake Yee came bounding up the stairs and grabbed me and whisked me right back into my own room.

"How is getting angry and getting back at her going to make your feel any better?" Jake Yee brought me to my bed and spoke into my clavicle. The sheets below us were soft and loving.

"This was your idea to begin with," I fumed.

"She's getting back at us for getting back at her for her parents being racist."

"What the *hell* are you talking about?"

I realized Jake Yee was on top of me, on my own blue bed after he had brought me back to my room. He realized it too and scanned my body quickly and I felt a surge of something but I shoved him off.

He laid down next to me and propped up his hand on the side of his face. "Want to play spin the bottle?"

"Get off of my bed!" I yelled and he slithered down to the ground. He stood up and brushed himself off.

"So, I guess we're just hiding out waiting for them to stop screwing around so you can what? Attack her?"

"No," I said, exhausted. "We just need to bury the hatchet. No more games. I can't believe I fell for yours to begin with."

"Sometimes you learn something from a game. Isn't that the C-Drama way?"

"Whatever," I breathed. I got up and Jake Yee followed me cautiously as if I were a bomb ready to detonate. Lady burst from the room, in Stills's oversized Lakers jersey and she glared at me.

"What," she said. I raised my eyebrows.

"What?" she screamed.

"I'm sick of you…what was the word Jake used?" I buckled my hips.

"Yellow-washing," Jake said, popping in, "That was my term."

"Exactly!" I went on. "I'm not Indonesian. I'm just a regular brown-colored Black person. I hate that your parents said that n-word equivalent so much."

"I stopped the relationship! I was weak before when I… um 'yellow-washed' you!"

"I just hate it all, Lady," I said, "You don't know how much it's wearing on me." Lady looked to Jake Yee helplessly and he shrugged, not taking a side.

She breathed in and out and slumped her shoulders. I felt tired too and I let my body loose as well. Jake Yee reached out and touched both of our shoulders. "Hey. Isn't everyone kind of racist?

We shrugged him off. Lady looked over at Jake Yee and her eyes flashed.

"So you and Jake are together?"

"You like him?" I challenged her. Jake Yee bounced up, near excited.

"Fuck no," she said. "I've BEEN with Stills. He's my sayang. He just didn't tell you."

I wildly looked over at the room and started to sizzle with anger and near run in to confront Stills, but Jake Yee popped out and gently placed his hands on my shoulders. He kept them there, a little too long and for a second, I just let him because I was tired of stupid things like intercultural racism and friend betrayals and mind games and C-Drama knock offs and I suddenly just wanted to write my dumb little puns in my Giant Eagle office. Take a page out of my book and leaf.

I slipped out of Jake Yee's grasp and went to the stairs. I leaned my head on my hands and I heard Lady sigh. She wrapped her body around mine too. I bristled, broiled, but then finally just let her hug my back. Jake Yee was in Lady's room hollering at Stills to put his clothes on and then the guys were out too watching this lopsided hug. Jake Yee started to make a stupid joke, but Stills pinched him and then we just were, being our strange selves, for some time not thinking about color or trauma or fear or parents or want.

The trash trucks were rumbling along, collecting the chair that reserved the parking spot. I could hear all of these things through the brick walls and hear Lady's soft breathing and Jake's black-lunged cough.

"Y'all want to smoke?" Jake asked.

We followed him out to the porch. The Pitt students trudged unhappily through the snow and the porchlights shuddered. We could hear the hum and screech and roar of cars going down Fifth Avenue. Lady and I stared at them as she snuggled with Stills under a downy blanket. Jake Yee rested against the railing and smacked his lips. I burrowed into the sofachair someone had brought out. Jake Yee looked at me, I looked at him, and he winked, slowly. I considered winking back but instead gave him a flash of teeth and looked the other way. One bird can't make a pun. But toucan.

The black city chattered, chattered all of its lies and jokes back to us, and we released our fears into its shimmering face.

7

Romeo Must Die (Again)

In Pittsburgh, it was summer sometimes, spring occasionally, but somehow always, always winter. By the time Jake Yee and Lady and I lived together the steel workers had largely lost their jobs or moved on, but we could still smell iron-piquancy in the Oakland air. Jake Yee and I were having black coffee on the porch of our three-storied rowhouse. He was smoking aggressively as usual, and we stared, exhausted, at Pittsburgh slush-thick street. Everything looked bleak.

We watched the rain on the sidewalk fall lushly and didn't say much.

Jake had received a call earlier that his father wanted him to take over his family's computer-something-something business in Hong Kong, and he didn't want to go, so he told his father off and now they were on bad terms. Secretly, I was happy he was staying with me and Lady after losing Benedict so easily without any more correspondence from him. It was weird to admit that I enjoyed Jake Yee's company. I didn't want him to leave forever.

Jake Yee barreled through a pack of cigarettes and sat quietly for most of our morning time until he looked at me swiftly and said:

"So, I have a question, Adrienne."

"Shoot," I said.

"How come they never remade *Romeo Must Die*? It's been enough time. They literally made all those 9/11 movies two years after 9/11 and they can't do *Romeo Must Die* again?" he said. I nearly fell over in my chair. All the stuff was going on with his dad and he was talking about a movie from eight years ago?

"Yeah, I've thought about that myself."

"Really?"

"Yeah. I have."

"Weird minds think alike," he took a puff of his cig.

"Anyway, it's probably because Aaliyah died and she's an icon so it would be pretty hard to fill her shoes," I offered, sipping my coffee. It was too hot. I placed it down on the table.

"I guess. They should do it anyway though. It was one of my favorite movies but the Asian guy never gets the kiss at the end! They have all this build up and then they just hug it out. It's messed up. He did all these cool kung fu moves for her and he never scored."

"The Asian guy always gets the girl in C-Dramas," I tried. "In fact, he often gets multiple girls. There are usually antics."

"I'm not talking about the Barbie Hsu-land where you live. I'm talking about American movies."

"Yeah. But I mean it's not like it was faring much better for Black women in American media. Back then. Or ever."

"Yeah."

"I heard Aaliyah didn't kiss Jet Li because her family died in the movie so it would be fucked up if they just started making out afterward."

"Then why bother to call the movie *Romeo Must Die*? Why even use the allusion to Romeo and Juliet if they're not going to address it?"

"Yeah."

"I heard it was because test audiences didn't like seeing an Asian man and Black woman kissing. It was too much for them in 2000. Ten years ago! I heard they did two versions and the one they chucked was the one with the kiss. Where is that footage? I mean that's gotta be precious footage now."

"Seriously? I'd love to see that."

"This is the same thing that happened in *Ninja Assassin* with Rain. The Asian guy does all of this fancy shit to save this Black woman and they don't do anything interesting."

"It's not like she owes him anything, though."

"I know. It's just like…you get what I'm saying though? Every white movie they always hook up. It's fucked up. Both of those movies were written by white guys."

"'Murica."

"Let's remake *Romeo Must Die*. Who plays who?"

"Nobody plays Aaliyah."

"See, people like you are why this wasn't remade, Adrienne."

"No let's remake the movie," I said. "Let's do it."

"Ok, some Some Actress and Some Up and Comer Who Looks Like Me are in a blah blah turf war about something something something, insert the hood, guns and kung fu. Anyway Dashing Taiwanese Guy and Aaliyah-lookalike fall in love and do awesome moves together and make out and fuck and live happily ever after. That's my movie."

"Okay, what if we set it in the future and it's actually the CHILDREN of Jet Li and Aaliyah's characters who are the main characters? Then we get out of having to get an Aaliyah-lookalike and skip having one more reboot in the world."

"That's fine. I still like my movie," he said and I finished my coffee.

"There's got to be a lot of great kung fu in it regardless. And the Black woman should get to fight too, not just be rescued," I said.

"Fair. My favorite scene was where this Chinese woman attacks Jet Li in a back alley or something and then Aaliyah is with him. He doesn't want to hit a girl so he gets behind Aaliyah and manipulates her arms and legs so she beats the shit out of the other woman and he doesn't have to. It's really cool."

He started his third cigarette.

"That's your favorite scene? A man beating up a woman through a woman?"

"It's romantic! And exciting. Have you no sense of romance?"

"I love romance. I just don't remember that scene."
"Pshaw. Okay, look, get up."

I stood up, cautiously. Jake Yee unfolded his longer body; he was at least 5'9, which was still much taller than the 5'1 me. He patted my shoulders.

"Loosen up. I'm not going to do anything to you. Why are you always so fucking guarded?"

"Because I don't know if I trust you."

"Ditto. Let's just pretend for like a second that you trust me."

"Okay."

He pressed his cold arms against the length of mine. He took my hands in his and made a fist over my fist. He pulled my arm back and brought it out into a punch. I felt his chest pressed against my back. I heard him swallow and my pulse flew around my body. Fucking Jake Yee.

"See?"

"I see," I said and broke from him, my heart still banging around. I sat back down and reached for my coffee.

"I don't feel like Aaliyah was honest about her feelings at the end of the movie," Jake Yee said. "I think she wanted to kiss Jet Li, but she was too scared."

I looked at a student struggling over a snow hump. "Who knows. Don't you hate kung fu?"

He pushed his face next to mine and I could feel the smoke from his breath on my lips. I blinked rapidly and turned my head to look away, but changed my mind and looked back at him. Against my better judgement, I leaned forward to kiss him and his lips met mine, not like the time when we were pretending with Lady. It was soft, brief, lovely.

He said gently, "And that's how the movie should have ended. Sequel next."

"Maybe."

"Is that a yes-maybe or a maybe-maybe?"

"A maybe."

Jake Yee sat back in his chair, smiled to himself and took a puff of his cigarette. "Good enough."

I let out a breath and smiled small.

8

Batman in Pittsburgh

Jake Yee took me, Stills, and Lady to the Korean Central Church of Pittsburgh, even though he was Taiwanese, not Korean. He told us he liked the vibe and they welcomed him more than the Catholic church he went to growing up. As we were walking out of the wide white doors, a soaring song followed us and we didn't know what the hell anybody was saying, but we saw Batman punch Bane clean in the jaw right in front of us.

The Dark Knight Rises had come to Pittsburgh and the city was abuzz. The Heinz Stadium was rented out for the movie, and Jake, Lady, Stills, and I almost went to the North Side to catch it but the traffic was too bad. I forgot about the Batman movie when it was finals time, but that was all the news could talk about.

Jake, Lady, Stills, and I exited the church as a stream of pious Koreans chatted in circles on the wet lawn, staring at us strangely. Some of them clutched my hands on the way out and I clutched theirs back. Some talked to Lady disparagingly, some loved her. Some of them cut their eyes at me darkly, like they didn't know why a Black American girl would be at the service in the first place. Jake Yee didn't interact with anyone, but I was still pretty excited about him inviting me to the church. I was reflecting on the general warmth the church had shown me as a guest, when Jake Yee grabbed my arm and said, "Adri…"

"What?"

"Batman."

"Oh my God!" Lady squealed.

"Shit," Stills said. I didn't see anything.

Jake Yee pointed past St. Paul's, which consumed Korean Central in its shadow. On the other side of the road was CMU's Mellon Institute, with its long beige pillars and high assembly of polished stairs. In front of this swept building, an enormous, armored Batman in full gear popped out behind one of the pillars and clocked a man with a mask and wire-shaped talons across his mouth. Folks were fighting around him, but Batman was center stage. Bane punched Batman back, and the director screamed "Cut!"

The brown, armored Tumbler was sitting out front of the building. It wasn't the one from the slick Keaton films. This was one looked military-heavy, huge. Jake Yee leaned down and gestured for me to get on his back so he could carry me the rest of the way, as he sometimes did. I jumped on. Lady frowned. He ignored her, shuffling forward, straight past St. Paul's and facing the Mellon Institute.

"Adri," he said, as I flopped around on top of his long back. "That's fucking Batman."

"That's fucking Batman," I said.

"That's fucking Batman in Pittsburgh," Stills said.

"It's fucking Batman in Pittsburgh," I said.

"Guys, I do NOT care about this. Can we go?" Lady said.

"Did you like church?" I asked Jake Yee, watching Batman get back up after Bane kneed him in the stomach.

"It was fine. I fucking love God, but nobody does anymore and they can all suck my dick."

"…Right…."

"Sorry," he said and shifted me around. "You're the preacher's girl. Maybe you can be a prodigal child and return back home. To my Korean church."

"I dunno. I've developed a mouth," I countered.

"Now. That. Is. true," he said and shook me on his back.

My father was a preacher for a reconciling Methodist church at one point; he taught me how to be a "good girl" which I didn't understand, but then he descended into alcoholism, lost the church and now largely worked random computer jobs at home, but sure, I was a preacher's girl. My Mami was constantly poised to leave, frustrated with him now that I was finally in college and she didn't have to stay around for me, but I just let it all go.

We neared the filming site and Jake Yee wrapped one arm around me to keep me secure and he waved his thin free hand back and forth.

"Dark Knight! Batman! Hey!"

I leapt off his back and slammed my hands against his mouth.

"You do know they're filming, don't you?"

"I want to be in the movie," he said.

"They don't want you in the movie," I said.

He shrugged and threw his hands in his pockets. Stills started punching the air. We watched them trade blows and takes and blows until everyone was tired and finished.

"Damn, that was so cool," Stills said, sucking his teeth, his eyes bright. He looked like he was pretending he was Batman himself.

"I don't think it's all that cool. A grown man in a Halloween costume," Lady said. "Who would wear that in real life as a vigilante? Christian Bale is pretty hot without all that shit on his head. He should just be himself."

"But then he wouldn't be Batman," I offered. "He would be Christian Bale."

She played with her lips. "Who cares?"

We lingered at the edge of the street, watching the actors play out their roles. Batman flew off the stairs and jumped in the Tumbler after Bane disappeared. We cheered for him, along with a new crowd that had formed, watching the movie.

"Nothing cool like this ever happens in Pittsburgh," Stills said, his eyes on Batman.

"Pittsburgh is plenty cool," Lady said. "I love it."

"Pittsburgh is Pittsburgh," I said. Jake Yee clapped as a stuntman dressed as Batman pulled off and stopped after a few blocks as cameras followed the car.

"Pittsburgh is Pittsburgh," Jake Yee repeated. "Have you ever thought about why they picked this city for this movie? It's dark and cold and everyone is just shuffling around trying to figure out where to go. It's depressing and gray and nobody knows what the fuck is going on. Even Batman. It's a perfect place to get plowed through by Bane."

"Batman thrives in darkness," Stills said suddenly. I glanced at him, not knowing he was a comic book fan.

"Sure," Jake Yee said, his eyes following the vehicle backing up. "But he doesn't want that darkness. It's just in him. Because his parents fucking died."

"Your parents are alive. You can't relate to Batman," Lady pointed out.

"I wasn't trying to fucking relate to him, *Lady*," Jake Yee spit.

He reached into his pocket and produced a pack of cigarettes. He pulled one out and balanced it on his tongue. "My parents might as well be dead anyway. You love your racist parents, Lady, but I *understand* that my parents are racist. There's a difference. Understanding versus loving. Anyway, I get Batman. He's stuck in the

'Burgh and has to fight all these assholes and for what? To save the city? Does the city care about him?"

"It cares," I tried.

He glanced at me quickly and looked back at Batman. "I hope so."

"You guys want to go somewhere after this?" Lady said, changing the subject.

"Primantis!" I offered.

"The tourist in her own city. Hey, little yinzer, you want a Steel Curtain shirt?" Jake Yee shook his box of cigs.

"Primantis is fine," Stills said and took Lady's hand. "So, we're going to the Strip?

"Batman would like Primantis," I said, striding toward the bus stop. "Y'all coming? Primantis is Pittsburgh."

"I agree," Lady said and it had been a long time since I smiled at her but I did.

"Pittsburgh is Pittsburgh," Jake Yee said.

"Pittsburgh *is* Pittsburgh," Stills said.

"No other way," I said, and they joined me at the stop.

9

The Con

We all went to FlowerCon in the sun. In that I mean, for the first time in a long Pittsburgh time, the clouds stretched open and the sun yawned out, making me and my friends happy-feeling, fresh and excited for life again. Pittsburgh's cold had a way of making you forget about the scent of spring.

The PPG Convention Center was hosting FlowerCon, one of the biggest animation conventions in the United States. It was the first time FlowerCon had come to Pittsburgh, and my friends and I, the Afro Otaku from my early college days and Lady Prananda and Jake Yee, all planned to go. My Afro Otaku friends wanted to come for obvious reasons, we were all dorks, but my roommates generally hated anime, Asian Dramas, and pop, unlike my core group. It was our last year and I had a plan to merge my friend groups. I thought it would be fun for us all to get to know each other. I hadn't seen my crush, the DDR-obsessed Benedict in some time and while I missed him terribly, I also felt as if he were the fixture of some distant life, some blessing of youth I was slowly growing out of.

When we arrived at the con, the Afro Otaku squealed. Lady Prananda and Jake Yee rolled their eyes, seemingly simultaneously. Lithe women, stout men in ribbons, femmes, non-binary folks in suits and tutus all populated the two-story space, wearing multi-colored wigs and holding katanas and ancient curved weapons. Nurses and mid-drift wearers and samurai all wandered joyfully through the halls. Bubbly, frenetic music bounced from the speakers and rows of tables were set up with artists.

Jake Yee scanned the spot, his eyes wide and intensely critical.

"I'm really trying to get this. Why you like this. I guess it works for me because you like this shit, but why? Everything is so fucking loud."

"It's fun. Kawaii. I dunno. It's just fun escapism to pretend you're in a fantasy world where your normal shit doesn't exist."

"Can I smoke in here? I'm gonna."

"Outside." He breathed out and left the cig behind his ear.

"I aligned with the Black kids at Schenley," Jake Yee said. "They were my allies. I was the only Asian kid at school, just like you were the only Black kid in your white ass school. I was always into hip-hop and my heroes were Black basketball players because I loved basketball so much. Fuck, man: Lebron was EVERYTHING. I didn't think my shit was interesting, and everybody knows about anime and Asian pop and all that shit, but I thought it was stupid. My sister likes it though. So, I was like OK. Whatever. But I'm trying to be in your shoes here. Like you see all of this Asian shit and you're like WHOA AMAZING but I'm like whatever. It's just loud and bright. Is that how you feel about hip-hop and Black shit?"

"I love hip-hop. I love Black shit. I'm Black."

"Jesus, Malcolm X. Well maybe it's different? I don't know," he watched two Black nerds dressed in *Naruto* outfits waltz by him. He saw white people dressed as Yusuke and Genkai from *Yu Yu Hakusho.* He gestured at a white and Black kid adorned with golden paint.

"Like look at this shit? What the fuck is this shit?" I heard an announcer coming from intercom saying that Fidelicia was going to collab with TM Revolution on the main stage. I pulled his shirt. "We have GOT to do this!" I said. "TM Revolution is huge…."

"No way, man," he said. He slid his eyes at mine. "Unless you *really* what me to come. With you."

"You don't have to but if you want to—"

He stared at me long and rolled his eyes. "Fuck it. I'm out."

"What?" I said. He shoved his hands in his pockets and shuffled away from me into the crowd. I thought about following him but didn't feel like dealing with his bullshit. He was always angry or making me feel guilty, for what? He was just a dour person. I went back to my business and skipped over to one of the panels to get a signature from two voice actors.

Somewhere between scooping up my autographs and moving to a *Neon Genesis Evangelion* voice actor panel, Elana found me and ran up to me out of breath.

"Hey, Adri. You're going to want to know something."

"What?" I said, concerned.

"Benedict's here. He's looking for you."

My heart skittered to a stop. A lightning bolt of joy and fear split me. Benedict. My Benedict. My first crush. Benedict in the peacoat, Benedict in the jazz club, Benedict in Dave & Buster's. He was here. I hadn't seen him in four years and he was back at the Con. Of course he would be. And I'd brought Lady, the Afro Otaku…how would he interact with us now that he and maybe I were potentially different? That I'd grown up a little bit? And there was that cursed Jake Yee.

I nearly choked. Jake Yee. No matter what they could *not* meet each other. Jake Yee would unveil the worst, searching parts of me to Benedict, and Benedict would think horribly of me. He would lose all respect for me. Damn it. I breathed out. It would be fine. There would be no way they'd meet each other.

"Also, Ferris is introducing Jake Yee and Benedict because YOU wanted us to merge groups," Dragon217 said and rolled his eyes. "I hope you're ready for that."

"Damn it," I swore as loudly as I could and the otaku around me bristled. "I mean. Holy hell! Where are they?"

"At Fidelicia's concert. We're all going to meet at the main stage," Dragon217 said.

"Okay, I'm there."

Fidelicia was known for her joy-making. She came on and we connected with her, felt our spirits rise up with hers. We were all fans. She was also known for her ardent anime addiction; she was perhaps the only lady rapper I knew who openly revealed her obsession. She rapped about anime, sometimes, and it was especially enthralling to see her perform with TM Revolution. She didn't have an opener and she walked right on stage, resolutely, with pink heels shaped like dragon mouths and a simple bra and pink panties. She opened her mouth and a cascade of raps descending from her lips; TM Revolution's guitars sizzled and soared.

Lady, Elana, Dragon217, and I stayed in our own group, cheering, as Benedict, alone, waded through the sea of Fidelicia fans. He was looking for us, but I was terrified to find him. It didn't feel like four years ago when I would have bounded over to see him, happily. I watched my former crush, hovering above the heads, looking for us. The old sparks fired off in my belly and I wanted to see him desperately and also run away. Then I saw Jake Yee awkwardly shuffle over to him. Jake Yee looked up and smiled at him. I shouldn't have told Jake Yee about Benedict when I first came to the apartment, when I was first nursing a young girl's heartbreak. My nightmare.

Fidelicia was doing her greatest hits with TM Revolution whose bassist made the guitar holler out in the background.

What happened next? I'd never had a boyfriend but now two guys I'd kissed were in the same room, hovering around me. I didn't know what the C-Dramas would tell me to do. I felt inclined to bolt. I hadn't done a thing wrong and neither had they, but I still felt intensely nervous and uncomfortable.

We reached Benedict and Jake Yee. Benedict was looming large over Jake, whose hands were typically in his pockets. Still, he was grinning up at Benedict, laughing with him. I neared closer, trying to hear them.

"Adri-chan," Benedict said, his eyes lighting up as he saw me approach. He reached out a hand to me but Jake Yee blocked it.

"Adri-*chan?*" Jake Yee repeated and he locked strong eyes with me.

I stared at both of them, helplessly. Jake Yee rolled his eyes and grinned up at Benedict. "So what do you think of this chic?"

"She's great," Benedict said, his soft eyes sweeping me. I nearly lost my breath seeing him again.

Jake Yee looked at me and rolled his eyes. "You got in his head."

Benedict raised an eyebrow. "Excuse me?"

There it was. The moment. The moment in which they clashed or hated each other or threw me under the bus.

Jake Yee glanced over at me, as if knowing everything. "She is great," he said, saving me. "Adrienne, we were talking about Fidelicia. Seems we're all fans. I think I'm even one too."

I smiled at Jake Yee, thankful suddenly for him. He could be an asshole but he certainly knew how to diffuse a situation. (That he might have created, but oh well.)

Benedict switched his eyes from me to Jake Yee. Something strange, nearly unreadable, flashed across his face and he looked at the concert, strongly. "I'm enjoying the show. It's good to meet new people."

"Yes," I said, relieved.

We huddled together and yelled for Fidelicia. We instead heard loud sound, anime colors, rapid noise. Hot blue and neon-pink flew out of the ceiling and covered us all. Our cheers lifted up, louder and higher until we could no longer hear our own voices.

Commercial Break

Writing Fiction

It was autumn, a few months into the first semester at Prairie Woods Nursery. The rich, maple'd winds flung ruby leaves from skinny maples.

The children were out. They rang around the rosy and tossed about flying balls and leapt into each other's arms and laugh-cried. They jumped into piles of shallow leaves, they slid onto tiny plastic Huffies and revved up, revved down. In their Own Worlds, they created and imagined, dreamed wild fantasies of pirates and princes and elfin journeys up high-tipped mountains. They painted Worlds and pushed away nasty truths like Mama never picked them up on time or Daddy was always seen Off with Some Woman. They played by themselves at first, then things got lonely. Too lonely.

So they stuck in friend-clusters, they shook hands and then, at some point they wondered, wondered about the Other Worlds where kids bounced and played differently. They started reaching for each other's Worlds, crushing into them, complimenting them, they transform into a flailing princess in One World, a monster in the next.

A little girl in the corner gets quiet. She doesn't speak out as much as the other children and wonders if anybody will see her World. Wouldn't that be too good to be true? That another child would enjoy the way she can make a frog laugh or she can color a horse or ride a rainbow. For a little while, she waits, waits, and she finds herself passed over by the other children. Finally, finally, just as the sun is flattening over a bloom of purple evening cloud, she sees another child approach. The child enters her World easily, is fascinated by how she colors that horse and that child rides the rainbow too. The girl becomes joyous beyond belief, and she forgets about the children who passed her by, who were finding their own Worlds to love, who were painting their own animals with their baby minds.

As more and more children come to say hello to her World, she remembers how lonely things could get, and she wants to reach for them all and bring them to her chest and tell them how lonely things got. So she says the small things that bring little smiles and while they are playing, she bends a flower petal with her baby mind. Despite the clamor of happy voices, she knows the way she bent that flower was reserved only for her.

OAV

The Vampires of Pittsburgh

PART 1

Shanus, a vampire living comfortably in the smoke of a steel mill coven, awoke in the trash in Lawrenceville. He was no longer a vampire.

The last thing he remembered was Dominique, the coven's head, instructing him to possess a woman named Paige Dalton who owned a burgeoning coffee shop and bookstore on Butler Steet. She was light brown-skinned and blonde, biracial and freckle-specked, a former "exotic dancer" who had spent her life struggling with depression. She had recently gone through some kind of awakening and now her energy, supposedly, had shifted, and she was a bright-toothed woman, who was always happy and uplifting communities, all that shit. Dominique wanted her to join the coven, thought Shane could get into her mind, find her weaknesses and convert her through the blood pact, or rather "possessing" which was basically just biting her neck. Shane used to be stationed in Spain but, after a few misadventures, he followed his coven leader Dominique to the Steel City mills. His mission for the night was simple; slip through the walls of Paige Dalton's room, float over to her neck, suck her blood, enter her mind, get her soul to agree to death and rebirth as a demonai. She would perish from the world but awaken, alive and bloodless and wild.

Dominique thought she deserved eternal life, sure. Shane didn't care. He just followed orders in exchange for a place to sleep. But tonight he had done the work he usually did, he'd flown to the second floor of her shop Le Bean, parted through the wall and leaned over to possess her while she was sleeping. He could feel the writhe and wiggle of her dreams, could feel the spurt of darkness twisting out of her mind that he could grab upon, exploit. Take apart. While he entered her mind-energy, ready to start working and tossing things about until he knew her too well, an invisible forcefield shoved him from her body, through the wall. He didn't remember anything else after that. Except now he was in the trash.

And, apparently, he was human.

The thing about being human was it mostly involved feeling weak. Shane groaned, feeling a weight on his chest, pressing, pressing but he didn't know a thing about it. He glanced around and saw a body, new, olive, and gleaming, propped up on flattened boxes. The trash around him was piss-wet, the banana peels and tomato halves rotted by his ear. He tried to prop himself up but the weight pressed him back down. Was he still alive? He lifted an arm, with effort. It was laced with heavy muscle, but it was smaller than his previous form. As a vampire he stood nearly 8 feet, was colored a thin gray-blue and he had an impressive mouth of sharp, elongated teeth. When Dominique possessed him, his form changed, unlike many of the other demonai who remained in forms that resembled their human selves, outside of a set of sharp fangs. But Shane changed, and Dominique never explained why. Shane didn't remember life before possession—most demonai memories were erased—so he didn't know what he looked like as a human. He loved his most ferocious demonai form, thought it made him intimidating to humans, terrifying and true and he guessed that it contributed to his high possession rate. Now, all he saw were long, bronzed human legs, hidden feet, a strong torso consumed by that oversized robe. He lay back down. Shit. Now what? He was alive, yes. He could feel a flush of blood rip through his fingertips. He didn't need to survive on blood or gobbling up spirits anymore. Shane knew what all demonai knew above all else---hatred for humans, and a practically nationalistic love for what he was.

And now that was all gone.

The question stuck in him like a heated thorn: why? *Why?*

Paige Dalton had a bad night. She dreamt of leaping purples, wet greens and an ancient, mythical scent, like burning sagebrush. A form emerged from a wall of fire, cloaked in blue-black and screamed little itchy things to her. When she dreamed, sometimes she saw faces: of her father before he passed, of her mother's spotlight-white face, the daughter she aborted, the ledge she thought to jump off after the last family member of hers died. She'd received moderate enjoyment from making folks joyful as a stripper, regardless of what folks said, but it wasn't for her either. So after a period of waiting (and, of course, the ledge and the dead daughter) she went to rehab, found a new life in Lawrenceville. She inherited her coffee shop from her sister and she pledged to make it a place of kindness and warm feeling. She often remembered these scraps of past in her dreams. Then she remembered the beautiful things: the mysterious woman who wrenched her back from the ledge who she never saw again, the community she found who came to her sister's shop, the projects she worked on with local activists and spiritual leaders. She had found herself anew, but still. Nights like last night were few but still present.

She ran down the stairs to the first floor of Le Bean and threw on an apron from the backroom. She went through the normal preparations for the day: checking in with the cook to make sure his pastries would come on time, some quick bookkeeping, starting up the coffee machine, lightly balancing the books. At the cashier was Flora, a Black Cuban girl who was in her gap year between high school and college. She adjusted small glasses on the bridge of her nose. Paige had employed her after she finished high school, and she was easily one of the smartest people she'd ever met. Flora was on her way to MIT for computer engineering, but she needed money, so Paige had set her up with a job at her shop. Paige raised a quick hand to Flora, who was cleaning the espresso machine. Flora smiled back.

"You look exhausted, girl," Flora said. "But beautiful. But exhausted. Beautifully exhausted."

Paige smiled and rubbed her temples. "I'm sure I don't look great. Sleep was a beast last night. I felt like I was wrestling with spirits. All that."

"Maybe you're thinking too hard about the reading on Friday," Flora offered. The group was bringing in a nationally recognized poet to read at the coffee shop, and he was bringing with him members of the Pittsburgh Arts council who were considering giving the coffee shop a grant. Everything had to go perfectly, and Paige's brain had been spinning, hoping to coordinate the rides.

"That's possible," Paige said, emptying out the trash from the night before. She wiped her hand with her face, excused herself, walked outside, and took a left to get to the alley where she usually tossed her trash. Without noticing where she was looking, she reached back, released the black bag and it hit something foreign, hard. She heard a loud groan and a "Shit!" and she ran over to the trash.

She got on her tip-toes, peeked inside and sure enough it was a man. Tanned, mestizo-looking with black hair thrown in his eyes. He was surprisingly muscular, as if he had trained at a gym regularly. Still, he was covered in a long, ragged coat that near consumed the trash.

"Oh my goodness," she said. "I'm so sorry! I'm getting help. Are you okay?

The body lifted itself, fell down. It lifted itself up again and the man threw his arms around the side of the bin. He stared at her, near viciously, and she recoiled. Then his gaze darted around, then it got pinpoint sharp, with some kind of darkness.

"You," he said hoarsely, then he collapsed. She ran back inside of Le Bean, to fetch Flora, or maybe call Dr. Carol or Father Ferguson, who could help her lift this huge man.

All she knew was she needed help.

When Shane awoke, he smelled the underbelly of a lavender petal. A thin scent, but it was stark, engulfing. He shivered, lifted himself on sturdy, new, strange arms and snapped open his eyes. Paige Dalton was at the foot of his bed, crouched over, her head tucked down, as if in prayer. She mumbled to herself and let out a long breath.

He closed his eyes again. What the fuck was she doing here? Where was he? He peeked one eye out and saw he was in a small domicile with warm-washed oaken walls, yellow flapping curtains, and a long dresser. He was planning to go back to sleep when Paige Dalton looked up, startled. She got to her feet.

"Hello, sir," she said. "You're up! Thank goodness. I was worried about you. I was worried you might not be alive."

He cocked an eyebrow and sat up, saying nothing. How was it possible he had been so close to her, and been so intimate, in her damn mind and to her, he was a vagabond stranger. He wondered his face looked like. That fucking heart again. *Badump.*

"We got you fixed up," she said, gesturing toward his chest. He looked down and saw layers of ACE bandages around his pectorals. He apparently hurt himself on the descent even though this body felt baby-new.

"There's a doctor who comes by in the mornings for muffins, I asked him to take care of you. Nothing too serious, he said. Just a few scratches and scrapes. How long were you in there?" Her huge eyes kept blinking up at him and he felt a weird sensation, something electric, near nauseating, like when he had first encountered her neck, when he was first thrown through the wall and into the trash. He suppressed it and tasted the tiny teeth in his mouth, much smaller than his fangs. The canines barely had a bite. She was speaking English to him; he was still in Pittsburgh. He could try speaking another language to her to confuse her, since she only knew English as far as he had researched, and he knew most languages fluently in demonai form.

Instead, he said, "You're not afraid of me." It confused him. She should be afraid. Maybe he didn't look intimidating enough.

But he could feel his body; it was much larger than hers, even though she was a tall woman. He was a man as far as he knew in a patriarchal world made up by patriarchal humans and here was a woman, picking a potential threat up from the trash, keeping him in her carefully swept place. Strange, she was. And not the dour person he had hoped to find based on Dominique's assessment.

She laughed gently. "I'm not afraid of anything. Sometimes you see so much, you don't get surprised. Sometimes you've been in so many shoes you know how they all fit."

He scrunched his eye. She should be easy to read, but she wasn't. She was just layers of barbed wire now, now that he'd lost his previous identity and could no longer enter her mind. Even if he did have access to her mind, it would just frustrate him further. Why the hell did Dominique want to possess her?

"What's your name?" she asked.

He shook his head.

She got a little closer to him and he inched away. "You don't have one?"

He instinctively was about to say Shanus, but bit it back. She heard the first half of the word and said, "Shane?"

Sure, he thought. Close enough. Too close. Whatever. What priest or priestess would guess that the great Shanus had been neutered. He nodded.

"That's a wonderful name! Shane," she repeated. He kept staring at her, wondering how long she would stay there. He suddenly wondered how the hell he was going to get back to the coven. What would he tell Dominique? Would he even tell Dominique? His stomach flipped. If Dominique knew he turned human, he might kill him, thinking he knew too much. It was better he stayed on the DL until he could be possessed again.

"Where do you normally stay?" she said.

Yes. He needed a place to stay for now. Where could he stay? Humans were so terrible to humans without homes, he didn't expect much from them. But at least he had a bed and room now.

"Nowhere," he said. She beamed, visibly happy he was talking to her.

"You can stay here for as long as you need," she said. "This is an extra room I just use for friends or storage. We're a nice community here. We have readings and hang outs. We have potlucks too. You can join whenever you'd like or not join. It's really up to you."

He scanned the boxes in the room. "Okay. I'll stay. Then I'll leave at some point."

She grinned and nodded. "That sounds good to me. Do you need a caregiver for the shower? I can get someone to—"

"No," he said curtly. He started to sit up, but this new body ached from something he couldn't define, and he fell back down. He let out a breath of frustration. Fucking human body. Maybe some priestess or priest he'd battled had put a curse on him in revenge for all the people he'd possessed. Or maybe it was something else related to this Paige woman. Regardless, he had to find out so he could get his original body back and return to the coven. As long as this body would just work right.

"I'll leave you," she said. "I just wanted to introduce myself. I'm Paige Dalton. I'm the owner of Le Bean on Main. I'm a friend of yours now that you're under my roof. Anything you need, I got you."

He opened his mouth, closed it. "Okay."

He tried to get up again. This time he was moderately successful; he swung his legs around and started dismounting from the bed but nearly fell again. Paige shot up and helped him up.

"You're okay," she said, her hand, bare-nailed, on his chest. He could smell lavender again. It must have been her shampoo. He didn't know if it sickened or calmed him.

What would a human say in this situation? Thanks? For putting him up, a random human in an industrial dumpster, indefinitely in her place? It was ridiculous to do so. Most humans wouldn't, and he knew humans well after playing with their brains for so many years. Shane wasn't really a person who said thanks very often, but this new body felt so much, so much faster than his old body. Heartblood, dulled senses, spiking emotions, weird gratitude, these were all human traits he normally kept even or non-existent as a demonai. This fresh brain gave him constant confusion, he kept trying to access that even-unfeeling part of his personality that he kept in the front as a demonai but he couldn't. He opened his mouth to say something, stopped himself.

Paige got up, smiled at him and said, "If you need anything else, just holler. I'll try to talk to some folks to get you set up."

"Okay," he said and watched the woman who had nearly silenced him, walk away.

Father Ferguson, now Blake Ferguson after he'd been excommunicated, felt a strong snap, then something stretched out in his body. He was sitting at his desk, answering a few phone calls when he felt that snap seize his chest, and he fell back in his chair. He breathed out rapidly, gripped the desk in front of him. At first he thought it was that strange surge of spirit—the GodSource—that gave him the abilities to see the world in acutely sharp colors, to battle demonai and bad spirits, to save others—acting up in his chest. But it wasn't the fresh flush he was used to. It was something different, something like a premonition.

The phone rang immediately and Ferguson considered not answering it but he picked it up anyway.

"News from the past. Blast from the past," said Anders, a priest from St. Gregory who had remained his friend even after excommunication. He was the only one who knew Father Ferguson had the GodSource, the Spirit given to certain priests that throbbed from the Relic, supposedly a chalice of Mary's tears. It was a near supernatural Spirit that filled a priest and allowed them to heal the afflicted, kill demons in spiritual or physical combat and undo possessions. Father Ferguson was given the GodSource many years ago but after the Vatican kicked him out, he pretended it was gone to avoid problems from them. It wasn't. He felt it still as powerfully as the first day he drank from the chalice of everlasting life.

In any case, when Ferguson thought about his previous times fighting demonai, it all sounded like some other dream life. Now he had a small, verandaed home in Aliquippa, a happy boyfriend named Edward who lived in Bloomfield, and a new community over at Le Bean where he would attend readings and help out unhoused people at Second Avenue Commons. He no longer fought nor stopped demonai possession and it seemed like God had given him blessings. And now there was this call. This strange and sizzling feeling.

"What's the news?" Ferguson said, near dreading it.

"Shanus is dead," said Father Anders. Ferguson nearly dropped the receiver in his hand.

"What?"

"The other priests haven't seen him around, neither has the diocese. They overheard, after stopping a possession, that Shanus hadn't been around..."

Father Ferguson was skeptical. Shanus was his nemesis: a huge, fearsome, sharp-toothed demonai who wouldn't go down easily. They had been battling each other for as long as Ferguson had been sent to go up against demonai. He could never kill or end Shanus and Shanus could never, for whatever reason, kill Ferguson.

"He likely just skipped town. He's been doing this for 500 years," Ferguson said.

"And he's very loyal to Dominique," Anders countered. "It doesn't make sense that he would just randomly leave."

"You really want to believe he's dead?" Ferguson said, wearily. At least if Shanus had left Pittsburgh, he would truly have found True Peace. He could finally leave the dark nights of the soul, the hauntings and the fights for innocents behind him, and he could focus on community building, his boyfriend. He was no longer Father Ferguson who battled demonai and had the GodSource, he'd just be Blake. "He probably just finally skipped town."

"Dominique is looking for him. He's nervous. That's not normal," Anders said. "Father Ward took out a demonai last night and he said that he was looking for Shanus. He never returned."

"We'll see," Father Ferguson said. They shared silly platitudes then Ferguson hung up the phone. He massaged his temples. He hated even thinking about Shanus. Maybe that's why the GodSource was acting up in his chest today. Stupid Shanus. Father Ferguson should have been the one to kill him, especially after the havoc Shanus had wreaked on his life. Especially after he had killed his first girlfriend Elsie, in another life, when he had just started out and left her to join the priesthood. Shanus simply did it to prove a point: he was more powerful. Shanus, out of all of the demonai, was plainly pure and unadulterated evil and he must be killed. And he wanted to be the one to do it.

Ferguson was a man of faith and forgiveness, supposedly, but he'd never forgive Shanus. He simply wanted him dead, just as Shanus likely wanted Father Ferguson in the ground. And now he was gone. So Ferguson could be at peace. He *should* be at peace.

Still, he felt unsettled. Whether it was the GodSource or Something Else, he knew to trust his intuition that all was not as well as it appeared.

Paige's week gradually went back to normal, despite the appearance of the new stranger. The stranger mostly stayed to himself and simply nodded when she brought him meals and clothes. She thought he'd open up eventually, but he was respectfully quiet to her and he kept his room and the bathroom searingly clean.

She also mostly concentrated on the task at hand which was bringing Wallace Woodrey to the coffee house as the main act and getting the schedule together for the open mic readers with Flora. Flora mostly ignored the man upstairs.

"He might be up to something," she said. "You should watch him. What are the chances he just randomly ended up in YOUR trash? What if he were trying to stalk you or something?" Paige wouldn't have it. "I don't feel that. In my gut. I just have to go with it."

To that Flora shrugged and went back to setting up the sheets. "Just know if he comes down and tries something at any point, he's done. It'll come from me."

Paige reached over and hugged the girl she often thought of as a little sister, even though this young woman was so much smarter than her in so many ways.

"I believe you," she said.

The evening of the reading, the space was set up with strings of burnt-red orange and coral lights, plastic seats were set up facing the stage and Flora and in addition to paintings of the Fort Pitt Bridge and Waterfront, she had placed candles on tables in front of the seats to create an intimate atmosphere. At around 7pm, folks sauntered in, hugging Paige and Flora, practicing their lines for the open mic, joining new discussions. Paige's former priest Father Ferguson drifted in with Edward, face long and haggard. She skipped up to meet them.

"Edward! Welcome. Father, you look exhausted. Have you been sleeping alright?"

"I'd say the same for you," he said, clearing his eyes. Edward rubbed his shoulder and Father Ferguson shook him off. "You also look tired, dear Paige. And you don't have to call me Father."

"Sorry, habit. And yes, I have been having rough nights. But we're all here and ready to party!" She pumped her fist. Father Ferguson smiled gently at her and touched her shoulder.

"You're a sweet one, child."

She smiled and led them to their seats. After That Woman had pulled her back from the ledge, she dropped her off at

Father Ferguson's parish. He helped her rehabilitate her life, find purpose, she was forever indebted to him. She didn't care if he was excommunicated and chose to live a free life; she loved him for all he was.

Once everyone was securely in their seats, Paige had about fifteen minutes left. She had been going back and forth about whether or not to invite Shane but decided to anyway. At least he'd have the invitation.

When she climbed up the stairs and entered his room, she saw him in the corner reading, wearing a black shirt that gripped generous muscles and simple soft black pants she'd brought him from a donation. He looked incredibly comfortable, and she was happy he was out of bed. She glimpsed at the book he was reading, and it was Sun Tzu's *The Art of War*. Of course, this mysterious man would.

"You like thinking about the dynamics of war?" she laughed. "My favorite: 'The supreme art of war is to subdue the enemy without fighting.'"

"Or, 'Let your plans be dark and impenetrable as night, and when you move, fall like a thunderbolt,'" he said quietly and shut the book. He looked up at her, awaiting the reason why she was there.

"Oh. I just wanted to invite you to a reading we're having downstairs. It's the community sharing their poems."

He shook his head. She nodded lightly, trying to mask her disappointment. "Alright."

"You're reading this book?" he said as she turned.

"Of course. That's why it's in this room. I like the premise. It's not all about fighting and pain."

"It's fine. Humans are cold-spirited and angry and mean and selfish and racist and evil. That's who they are. You learn to fight it. You win. You lose. There's an art to all of that. Protecting yourself, from them."

Paige turned back around. "Oh, Shane. I used to feel that way."

"Why don't you still?" he said, leaning forward slightly.

"Because people have a little piece of God in them, I think. As evil and cruel as they can be they're also capable of great love, compassion and most of all they are sacred."

Shane snorted. "That's naïve. But you're not naïve. You're not innocent. I know you aren't."

She winked. "You can tell? No, not even close. Shane, why don't you come down to the reading? Please? You can think we're cold and cruel and selfish but we'd love to have you around. In all of our ineptitudes."

They stared each other down; she felt his eyes sweep her blackly, and she stayed firm. She was used to these types, the inflexible ones who postured but were really broken somewhere. Just like she just once was, standing on that ledge.

"I'll come," he said, putting the book down. "I have nothing better to do. I'm at the very least curious at how you see the world."

"So you can destroy it?" she laughed and in that moment she had a slash of darkness in her voice she didn't mean.

He grinned. "We'll see."

She flashed her teeth at him. "Come along then."

When Shane joined Paige later, he noticed that the place was packed with guests. They milled about, chatted in chairs, snacked on cheese the girl Flora had brought out. He lingered at the bottom of the stairs as he scanned the rows of people, thinking this was surely a bad idea to expose himself to all of these people in this state. He was about to turn back and go up the stairs to his room when Paige saw him, her eyes brightened and she scurried over. She grabbed him by the arm and led him to a seat in the front of the crowd.

"You're our treasured guest," she said and he found himself obeying her against all of his better judgment. He squeezed his large body into the small chair and leaned forward. What the hell had he got himself into? He glanced around to check out all of these laughing humans, and out of the corner of his eye he saw a flash of red. It was a red he had been seeing for 40 years, throughout endless, infuriating quarrels that had no victor.

Shane whipped his head back around. Was this a trap? Had Father Ferguson and Paige set this up and they were both going to kill him?

He glanced at Paige going up to the stage and talking with the author, getting him water. Even that woman? He hadn't read anything about her or felt anything in her that indicated she had anything to do with the priests and priestesses who killed vampires and stopped possessions. He was fairly certain he knew her record, but she kept surprising him. Indeed, these humans weren't to be trusted.

As he was thinking these things and planning his exit, Paige came back around and sat in the empty seat next to him. "I'm really excited you're here," she said.

"How do you know that man with the red hair?" he said. "Who?" She turned around and looked behind her at Father Ferguson. She beamed. "Oh, that's my priest! Well, he was my priest before he got excommunicated. He's a sweetheart. He brought me back from the brink many times. I'll introduce you to him if you're interested!"

"No," he said flatly and looked back on the stage.

"Okay," she said. "Not everyone is for everyone."

She got back up and looked over the lineup one more time. He watched her long body reach and stretch and posture. She would be considered a beautiful human, he noticed. Her body measurements were shapely, her cheekbones high, and light brown skin flushed and joyful. Her blonde-brown hair was pulled back in a highlighted ponytail and she wore a green tee and faded jeans, nothing fancy. He tried to imagine her as the ledge woman who almost took her life but it was difficult to reconcile those two images together with the woman in front of him. The woman he was meant to possess was so fucking sprightly and joyful. It was all too strange. She occupied his thoughts and he hated it. He attributed it to the pulse and shake of this human body, how it got softer, got intense hits of feeling, the black of the sky fell through the window and haunted him, haunted him. He felt too much. And nothing.

He leaned back in his chair, and the various poets came up and tried to talk to him but he glared at them so they would leave. They still kept coming, some complimenting his shirt or muscles, other folks simply inquiring who he was and why Paige had taken him in. He didn't answer most of the questions, just stared blankly at folks and even then they talked to him. Fucking humans.

Flora eventually got up and introduced the first round of poets. Shane listened, more intensely than he thought he would. They emoted openly; some cried, some shouted. The poetry was performative, emotional, things Shane pretended to despise but he couldn't stop watching. Paige introduced the second round and they were also, as much as Shane hated to admit it, fascinating. As they discussed their flaws and pains, he knew he could get into their minds and destroy and possess them, but he didn't feel like doing so in this body. He just wanted to listen to them.

It was all so insane. Why did he care about listening to amateur poetry and why had he listened to this stripper woman? This stupid human body. He couldn't wait to be back in his previous form, when he was terrifying, unyielding. Right now, he was listening to a girl talk about her upbringings in the Bronx and the impact of the move when glass exploded behind him. An arrow with a heated tip shot through the glass straight for the back of Paige Dalton's head. Shane caught it, jumped up, and hurled it right back through the window. He knew exactly who this asshole was.

Everyone was screaming and Paige fell over in shock and Shane caught her. She looked up at him wildly, and he said, simply, "I'll take care of this."

He left her and threw his eyes at Father Ferguson. Ferguson, who was also on his feet, helping move folks to the second floor and looking at the hole. Shane didn't have time to worry about Ferguson. He jumped over a few overturned chairs and rushed through the door, out into the street. He saw that fucking Lias, with his grey shriveled-up body and stupid-ass crossbow. He was pacing back and forth pulling back an arrow to try again when Shane ran toward him and easily knocked him down. Maybe this human body wasn't so weak after all. He tried to wrestle the crossbow from him but Lias had some fight in him and he kicked Shane off.

He stood up, his eyes glowing red. "Who the fuck are you? You don't have a lick of the GodSource so I know you ain't a priest. Stay out of the way."

"I'm definitely not going anywhere," Shane laughed. "What the fuck are YOU doing? Attacking humans at a fucking poetry reading? What did you think would happen?"

Lias stopped. "Humans?"

Shit. Shane talked with too much familiarity. "You're an idiot. I'll need you to get out of here."

Lias narrowed his eyes. "I'd know that voice anywhere. Shanus, you picked a pretty face but that body is not going to be strong enough to fight me."

Shane spit on the ground. He didn't care if Lias knew who he was. He was a perpetually shit-faced vampire who had no sense of power, so he just endlessly sucked the tits of those in power. The fact that Dominique sent Lias to find him was insulting. He could have picked that girl Gala, or Yemo, or Missy, who had gone up against one of the disciples back in the fucking Biblical era, or that new vampire from Nigeria he heard was pretty powerful. All of those folks were close to or in Pittsburgh and Dominique had sent *LIAS*. So much for being Dominique's right-hand man.

Lias lunged at Shane and Shane dodged him. Lias fell over behind him and Shane sliced at his stomach; Lias doubled over. He fell to the ground, then got back up, retrieved his crossbow and brought his arm back to unleash another arrow. Loser. He had one fucking move. Shane tossed him over his back and got him to the ground, wrestled a few arrows off his back, and as he was about to successfully retrieve the crossbow, a flash of red blew in and grabbed it first. Of course. This day started out okay and got so bad. So fast, Shane cursed. Shane got to his feet and faced Father Ferguson, who had a crossbow with zero bows and who faced Shane who had three arrows with heated tips.

"Hey," Father Ferguson said, and he put one hand up and slowly lowered the crossbow. "We're on the same side."

Shane stared at him, perplexed. He didn't recognize him? But Lias had? Whatever was happening, Shane decided to go along with it.

"I don't think we are," he said, despite himself. "In fact, I'm sure we aren't."

"You saved Paige Dalton," Father Ferguson said. "That means you're on my side. My only question is how much do you already know and how much do I need to keep from you?"

Lias got back up and he tried to grab Father Ferguson, but the former priest caught his arms and shoved him at Shane. "You've got the arrow," he said. "Right through the heart." As if Shane didn't know.

Lias kicked and fell and almost got out of Father Ferguson's grasp. Shane didn't have long. Shane stared at Lias, this asshole who he had known for at least 200 years. He was pathetic and annoying but here he was about to kill him. In fact, why was he even thinking about this? If he were in his previous body, he would have easily already ended this jerk. And then there was that stupid shop and those women. Shane raised his hand and closed his eyes and punctured Lias through the heart with his own heated arrow.

Father Ferguson dropped Lias's body and they both waited for it to disappear into air and float back to his soul-self. To Hell, or wherever dead demonai went;nobody really knew, even demonai. After he was gone, Father Ferugson stood back up, wiped his face. He looked back at the coffee shop, which now had all of the lights off, a broken window and a group of terrified poetry lovers crouching in darkness on the second floor.

"Shit," Ferguson said, as he walked away from Shane. "This is a complete mess. These guys usually stay under wraps, are pretty quiet. This is unusual for Pittsburgh demonai. Sorry," he said. "Forget I said a thing."

Shane stared at him. Father Ferguson's eyes slid over at Shane. "You're new at the readings. The new guy."

"Yeah," he said.

"I feel like you don't just happen to be new. There are a lot of strange things happening right now and I don't feel a six-foot-three hulking guy showing up to poetry readings is a coincidence."

Shane wiggled his eyebrows. He couldn't resist teasing Ferguson, especially since they were at the very least pretending as if they didn't know who each other was. Ferguson blushed. Then he waved a hand.

"You don't have to tell me who you are. But I know you're one of us based on your actions. And I know you're in on this. Because you saved Paige. And you killed Lias. And you didn't show one inch of fear when you faced that demonai. So, you don't have to like me, know me, or see me again, but just know, if you hate demonai and you save humans, we're on the same side."

Shane felt like gagging. He saved Paige? Saved a human's life? Had he? It was an instinctive reflex, as was covering her. He would have never done a thing like that in Shanus's body. He didn't understand it himself and preferred not to think about the reasons why he did what he did. But he would never be on Father Ferguson's side. The only thing he could think is it would be advantageous to keep up the ruse that he was Ferguson's ally. He obviously didn't have any demonai allies so he might as well have a human on his side who could kill demonai and would make sure they didn't come for him. Plus, he would get to know Ferguson better if he needed to kill him at any point and end their dance someday.

Shane turned and said over his shoulder. "You can do what you want. I'll do what I do. If we cross paths, that's fine."

Ferguson smiled. "Good enough for me."

Shane put out the last visages of fire on the arrows, tossed them over to Ferguson and walked back into the darkness, not knowing if he was coming back to that coffee shop in some time. For various reasons he still didn't understand.

Paige stood at the mouth of the open coffee house door with Flora. They had watched the most impossible battle and heard the most confusing things but at the very least they had protected the reading attendees and the readers. She saw Shane retreat from Father Ferguson and start striding away and she didn't want him to go. She thought it would be terrible if he suddenly left, with no community or friends, to be on his own. Like she could have at one point in her life. She knew the police would be coming whether she wanted them to or not and she knew that would be overwhelming to Shane, but she didn't want him to go. She asked Flora to look after the group and she ran out into the sidewalk. Father Ferguson shouted out to stop her, that it was all too dangerous and ridiculous right now, but she sped right past him and finally caught up with Shane.

Out of breath, she doubled over and clutched her knees. She folded her body back up and wheezed, "Don't. Go."

Shane stared at her; she couldn't read him. She didn't care. "Stay. You don't have a place to stay. You shouldn't be alone."

He smacked his lips, looked at Father Ferguson then back at Paige. "It's probably better I'm not here. For you."

She shook her head. "You saved my life. You protected everyone in that shop with Father Ferguson and you don't even know us. That deserves all of my respect. You're free to stay with me as long as you want. We'll take care of you."

Shane's staring got a little stronger and she didn't know what it meant so they simply looked at each other, as if trying to understand the other person and coming up against walls.

"Okay," he said.

She grinned. "You mean it?"

He didn't say anything. "Your window is going to be expensive to fix," he said.

"We'll fix it up ourselves. Even though we're poets and drifters everybody will chip in. I have no doubt about that."

"You have faith in them."

"I do," she said. "And in you too. You can help us out if you'd like. Might be something to do?" Shane shrugged. "Okay."

Paige knew not to prod any further, and when the police sirens came, she encouraged him to run to Father Ferguson's and hide for as long as he needed. Father Ferguson was behind them suddenly and he started to clamp a hand on Shane in encouragement. Shane retracted his shoulder.

Ferguson didn't notice. "I don't have a lot of room but sure. Feel free to crash at my place for the night before you realize what you want to do. I'm not exactly offering the indefinite housing though. I do have a boyfriend who is over pretty often."

The last thing in the world Shane wanted was to stay with Ferguson. And his boyfriend? Ferguson was actually attempting to live a peaceful civilian life? As if that could happen.

Shane waved a hand and sauntered back into the night. "You'll come back?" Paige asked his back. "I hope you will."

He glanced over at her. "Probably."

Paige knew he'd come back. She felt it strongly. And not just because he had nowhere to go.

Shane spent the night dodging shadows he feared were coming for him that turned out to be vague nothings. He lurked in bar corners, ignoring women and men and watching humans poison themselves with alcohol. They looked so happy, he thought, as he watched them. But weren't they also miserable? Isn't that why they were here on a Monday night? Looking for skin or drink or love? He watched a couple joyfully kiss in a phone booth set up inside of the bar, and he couldn't read them as easily as he used to. In his demonai body he'd see the length of their relationship easily. He had to; he was well-versed in jumping on human mind-lengths, manipulating humans, confusing them. But now he simply saw two humans looking like love. But they couldn't be? Could they?

He thought about the arrow going for Paige's head. How he'd reached for it, plucked it out of the air easily. He thought about Father Ferguson's comment about him "saving" her when he hadn't saved a human intentionally in his entire 500 years as a demonai. He wondered about this body he now owned, who it belonged to. His consciousness was in it, but he didn't know if it were somebody else's body, if it was who he was before he'd been possessed. There was so much he didn't know.

It was so much easier to be a demonai. He ached to have his old body again and the rich quiet of his head, the strategic single-mindedness of his goals: eat, kill, live, do it again. There was that knowledge, the absolute certitude that he was always right. About humans. About them being disgusting scourges. About the world around him. Now so much was confusing. Hell, he was confusing himself.

Shane didn't sleep that night, he simply wandered the streets of dark Pittsburgh. He crept into corners he used to hide in when he was a vampire, the snatch of black behind the bowling alley, the white brick next to a shadowed club. He eventually found a warehouse and slept there. The next day came and no new vampire came to claim him. He walked out of a warehouse, the sun blasting him in the face, speaking about new things, speaking about new fearsome things.

PART 2

Father Ferguson spent the next two weeks helping Paige rehabilitate Le Bean, navigate the media attention, and explain away footage somebody had caught on camera that wound up on the AOL chats and said "vampires R real!!" He got a call from the Vatican about the whole situation, which he ignored. They couldn't do anything to him. His only job was to protect the city of Pittsburgh, on his own terms.

Throughout the time he spent helping Paige, he tried to peek into the mind of the tall, musclebound man who Paige was caring for. He never offered much about his life, he randomly disappeared and reappeared, but he always came back to help Paige fix the window. He barely said a word to her; he simply held the ladder when she went to the attic or lifted boxes and organized signs, then he disappeared. He'd come back at night, sometimes in the mornings when Ferguson would come in before his new job at PNC. They'd all sit: Flora, the young girl, Paige, the man, and Ferguson, and drink coffee in somewhat comfortable silence.

Still, as the man was slowly ingrained in the group, his mysteries annoyed Ferguson. He felt like he was actively holding something back and carefully speaking. Ferguson knew he had at least some knowledge of the underworld, and perhaps was a stoically valiant vampire hunter with a long past. Ferguson wanted to befriend him. He didn't have the GodSource, but perhaps he was powerful and swift and practiced even in the flash of fighting he'd seen, perhaps somebody Ferguson could mentor and train. He always wanted to have a trainee to take over for him after the years of battling caught up to him and this man seemed fresh, strong and spry. Yet, he said nothing.

One morning, Paige closed the store in celebration of Flora nailing a standardized test. She insisted they all go down to Station Square and shop. The air was sharp-toothed and biting and nobody liked the idea, but they all ended up following Paige anyway as she drove them all down to the cold center of Pittsburgh.

Paige and Flora went to Kiku to look for knick-knacks and Ferguson and The Man lingered, a strong distance away, in the parking lot of the Freight House Shops.

"Hey," Ferguson offered. "You want to ride the incline? Have you ever? It's pretty fun."

The man shrugged and followed Ferguson to the row of scarlet cars slowly creeping up a slanted railway.

"Pittsburgh hallmark," Ferguson said, and he paid for them both to sit in a car. Luckily, nobody was in there with them, as it was winter, in the middle of the week, and the incline was largely unpopular during those times.

"Listen," Ferguson tried again. He sat on one end of the car, the man, with his hands in his pockets, sat on the other end of the cab.

"Yeah?" the man said.

"I know you know about my world. You know what I'm talking about. I want to help you. I want to train you. Maybe you were a former priest? I don't know. I was too. But I have the same mission. And I know you do too."

The man stared at him for a very long time. Ferguson looked back, near pleadingly. He didn't know why he wanted this man so much on his side. He felt something, perhaps it was the GodSource, telling him they needed to work together.

"What do you think?" Ferguson tried again. The man leaned an arm back on one of the railings and watched smudges of Pittsburgh bush streak by.

"Do you know my name?" he said.

"What?" Ferguson said.

"My name. Hasn't Paige Dalton told you?"

Ferguson tried to remember his name but he realized Paige rarely said it, she just referred to him as "you" and so did Flora. He thought he'd asked.

"What is it?" he said.

The man blinked and threw a long gaze at Ferguson then he looked, strongly, back at Pittsburgh. "It's Shane."

Ferguson heard him and didn't understand. "Okay."

Shane turned around and leaned two heavily muscled biceps on his knees. "You don't get it."

"I don't?" Ferguson said.

"Oh, Fergie. You always were so stupid," Shane said and then immediately Ferguson blinked once and knew. Only one being in the whole world called him Fergie.

Ferguson stood up frantically, happy he'd kept a small knife in his shoe. He reached down, retrieved it and balanced himself on the inside of the cart. Flashbacks of his time with Shane the entire two weeks streaked by and it all made complete sense. How had he not seen it?

"Are you fucking kidding me? How? How the hell did this happen?"

Shane crossed his legs, uncrossed them. He leaned back in the chair and grinned. "I have no fucking idea myself, Fergie. Woke up one day and voila! New body." He wiggled his torso, revealing a ripple of stomach underneath his black shirt. "It's a hot one though, do you like it? Nah, I hear you have a boyfriend."

The incline groaned up.

"Fuck you," Ferguson said. His eyes darted around Shanus's body trying to gauge whether he could weaken him somewhere. He was pretty sure Shanus didn't have a weapon on him so he had the advantage. Didn't he? He could never read Shanus well. But this new thing, person, being---this *Shane*---didn't know this body at all, he could tell. He noticed Shane flubbing around and running into things around Le Bean and attributed it to him just being a klutz. But now it was because he didn't understand his human form well enough. Perfect.

The incline had one more stop to go before it reached its final destination: the Mon Wharf.

"You're leaving that coffee house, Shanus," Ferugson said plainly, with his knife pointed. "Paige and Flora and that whole community are innocent. I know that means nothing to you, but it does mean that they are useless to you. You already got them involved in your bullshit; I knew you were connected to that arrow somehow. So, you're going to get out of here." Shane sighed slowly. "We're really doing this today?"

Ferguson grinned. "I told you. You're leaving that place. You are going back to the coven or you are going to die. You have two options."

"Oh, sweetie," Shane laughed. "I wish I could go back to the coven. But I can't. Because if Dominique finds out I'm human and killed one of his own, I'm dead anyway. So, I'm just gonna do my thing. You can do you."

"You piece of shit. You are endangering so many people with your mere presence right now."

"Nobody's a bigger piece of shit than you, FATHER FER-GUSON. Anyway," Shane raised his arms over his head and flexed his pectorals. "What do you really think you could do to me, baby? I'm HUMAN."

The incline rumbled to a stop and the doors slammed open. The two men strode forward, nearly fell into each other, and when they got outside the air threw itself at their faces. At the top of the Mon Wharf, the bumps and ridges and low cuts of the PPG building, the black Steel Tower jutting to the sky, the tan Grant, the multi-glassed PPG, the sprawling yellow bridges flew open below them. They walked briskly, pretending to be friends or lovers, to an open space. Nobody was around nor saw them; it was that cold. The sky reddened and pinkened with sunset.

"I don't care if you're human," Ferguson whispered into the iced wind. "You're going to die. And I'm going to be the one to kill you."

"Why? Just the other day you were giving me your room and recruiting me to the Super Team of We Got Kicked Out By The Vatican people that is completely comprised of the incredibly pathetic you."

"I left."

"Sure you did. You're practically nationalistic for the Catholic Church. You got chucked out."

"Says the guy always sucking your coven leader's dick. And he sent LIAS after you? LIAS? Jesus. I had to laugh."

Shane ran a hand through his hair. "I'm over it."

"What the fuck are you over? Killing my girlfriend?" Ferguson surged with hatred.

"Yeah," Shane challenged him, though Ferguson saw him wince. Why did he wince? What a strange expression to see on Shane's human face. Ferguson dismissed it. "I did. Your precious Elsie. Can your new boyfriend compete with our prairie girl Elsie? Does Edward know? Have you ever told him about That Girl you loved?"

Ferguson brandished his knife, a small blade from the Holy Land, it had an inscription burned in Lazarus's blood. He'd used it on Shane before to successfully ward him off.

"You don't have the GodSource, Shanus. You're nothing. You know it. You've come to nothing, and now you're just like us and you have nowhere to go so you prey on the weak."

Shane snorted. "Are you saying Paige Dalton and Flora are weak? Fucking sexist."

"You know what I mean. Keep their names out of your mouth."

"I'll say whatever the fuck I want to say," Shane said. Ferguson was tired of the usual pre-battle banter and he lunged at Shane with his knife, trying to beckon the God-Source but it wouldn't show up. Shane dodged the blows easily, looking surprised he did and Ferguson, pissed, caught him in his jaw. Ferguson was temporarily confident, ready to aim for the heart this time but Shane grabbed his arm wrenched it back, and wrestled the blade out of his hand. He kicked Ferguson, viciously, down and pointed the blade at his face. Ferguson, unfazed, looked straight back at Shane. How long had they been in this position? Pointing weapons at each other, yelling platitudes. And now they were both human. Still wasting their time.

"To quote you, Shanus, 'I'm over it,'" Ferguson sighed and started to move his face away from his own knife in Shane's hands.

"That's a really convenient thing to say when I'm about to kill you. It's like you saying 'Oh no I won't date Idris Elba.'"

"I'm good with this," Ferguson said. "Please get that blade away from me. Unless you actually are going to kill me. But you're stalling." He smirked and went on, "Or is it because you don't want to kill a precious human being? Like you protected precious Paige? Maybe you're getting a little human after all?" Ferguson didn't believe any of that but he knew it would rile Shane up and it did.

He pressed the knife against Ferguson's face and said, "You're pretty fucking confident because I'm human. But I'm the one on top of you right now. You do know I can end your life at any time. And I can. And best believe me, it may not be now but at some point, I will."

"As long as I have the GodSource, you can't," Ferguson laughed. He rammed his shoe into Shane's shin and Shane tried to ignore it, but in the moment, Ferguson saw an opening and tried again, getting the knife back and pointing it at Shane. Shane also, similarly, didn't seem to care.

"That's cute. And doesn't matter. Because I'm going to wind up with that in a second and next thing you know—"

"What the hell?"

The two men whipped their heads over and saw Flora with her eyes wide. She approached them both, slowly and said, "Why are y'all fighting?"

Father Ferguson scrambled to his feet and tried to reason with Shane with his eyes, but Shane's knife remained pointed at Ferguson.

"I thought y'all were friends?" she said.

"Not a good word for that," Shane said. Flora raised her eyebrows.

"Flora, get out of here—" Father Ferguson began but Flora raised a hand to stop him.

"This is an emergency. I don't know what the fuck is going on but Paige is gone. And she didn't just 'disappear.' I went to the bathroom and then she was gone. Like out of nowhere. And I'm not an idiot. Given the recent string of events from this guy," She gestured at Shane, "Appearing as our resident Stranger Comes to Town plus flaming arrows and the like. I'm thinking this isn't just apocalyptic randomness."

"They got her," Father Ferguson said almost immediately. It made sense. Paige was the one housing Shane, who to them, might as well be dead since he killed their own and switched sides. A part of Ferguson wondered even faintly, if Shane's humanity was reacting in some way to her compassion but he dismissed it. Shane, human or not, was a beast.

Shane ignored Ferguson and talked to Flora, "How much do you already know?"

Flora rolled her eyes. "I mean a fanged weirdo shot flaming arrows at us. Shane just 'powered up' and kicked his ass along with you, Father F. So, I'm thinking I'm living in some kind of vampire bizarro world or everybody is HEAVILY and I mean HEAVILY on drugs. But regardless of what's going on, we need to get Paige home safely."

Father Ferguson and Shane regarded everyone. Shane glanced at Ferguson and said, "I'm not doing anything with him. I'll get her back to her shop safely on my own. And not because I give a shit. It's because we don't need humans getting involved with us."

Flora's face did a *WTF* and she shook her head. "Shane, you sound crazy. We're doing this together. We don't do this alone. I'm good with computers, I'll hold the fort and tell you wherever we need to get in. I've got the hacking part down. We bust in…"

"I know the codes," Shane said simply. Father Ferguson just wanted to punch him off of the Mon Wharf.

"So where is she?" Flora said.

"At our coven. Somewhere in Dominique's place. He's the leader of the coven. He got her to lure Father Ferguson in probably."

"Why not Edward?" she asked. "What happens when a human gets captured?"

"You don't want to know," Shane said and walked a little faster forward.

"You're a vampire?" Flora said to Shane.

"Not anymore."

"Retired vampire? I've been reading about the weird shit going on in Pittsburgh on the blogs for some time. You know we have a *Vampires of Pittsburgh* website on Netscape but nobody gives a shit. Nobody cares."

"That's because it's on Netscape," Shane said.

Father Ferguson jumped in, "We're going."

Father Ferguson couldn't believe it, but Shane was already leading the way.

Paige awoke in a thick, shaggy black. There were stray streaks of blue and shimmering flickers of gold in the walls, but there was a bed and she was alone. She lived by herself, though she always had the company of Flora and now her new friend Shane. But this was a terrible kind of solitude, it pressed against her head walls and reminded her of other times, after she pressed her ass into a man's face for money, then went back upstairs of the club and opened up pictures on her phone of cute-cheeked babies online, fantasy girls growing in her belly. She remembered the time she found out she couldn't have that girl because her womb couldn't reproduce and the doctors told her she had to abort. She remembered the fast loss. She remembered the last day she wound and spun for men and watched them watch her, hungrily, greedily, as if she was something to own and capture. She never judged these men, thought they were simply tired souls looking for quick entertainment. She had a job to do, so like always, she did it. But that time after she lost her daughter, everything felt forced and exhausting. She wanted to not feel judged for what she had done, she wanted to live freely, without the haunting of that little face. It didn't go away, neither did the bad pain from her absent mother and all those things congealed to become the day when she left the club, in her most beautiful outfit, a g-string and heavy breast glitter and she performed one last dance then walked out.

They clawed for her but she kept click-clacking out. She drove and drove until she reached the frozen Allegheny River behind the riverwalk. She would simply jump in, drown herself. It was cold, and nobody would notice.

But then that girl wrenched her back. And brought her to Father Ferguson, a priest who was on his way out of the

Catholic Church. He gave her a home and then her sister came into her life again after finding out about the suicide attempt and gave her Le Bean; there was great kindness in her life. That made her believe in people above all the darkness and hate she daily encountered as a Black, biracial woman in America.

But now she was in a dark place again, remembering everything and she was terrified. Was she dead? Had some guy from the club finally found her after all these years? Had one of Shane's people (she suspected at least he was connected to some folks she shouldn't trust) taken her? Why was she afraid? Should she be afraid? She scanned the place and had no weapon to fight anyway. But she had her teeth.

The door opened and a long-bodied, middle-aged, willowy man with pale skin, night-black hair and a scarlet kimono gazed back at her. He smiled, faintly and stood in the halo of the door. "Paige Dalton," he said. "I've been wanting you to come to this coven for quite some time."

"Coven?" she said and noticed the man's fangs. They reminded her of the man she'd seen briefly in front of Le Bean that Shane had battled. "You're a vampire or something?"

"We prefer the term demonai."

"Holy," she said and leaned back against the bed, shivering.

"You weren't prepared for this," he laughed. "In any case, Paige Dalton, I don't want to hurt you. I'm not here to do anything harmful to you. I simply want to talk."

Paige looked wildly around her. If he was a vampire, weren't they immune to crosses? If only she had one of Father Ferguson's crucifixes.

"Okay," she said, slowly. "You can talk."

He came carefully over to her and sat on the other side of her bed. "My name is Dominique. I am the leader of the Pittsburgh coven of demonai. Our job is to possess humans, and in that I mean we draw their blood to enter their minds, convince them to say yes to their own death and at that point we convert them into demons with little fangs, which you call vampires and which we call demonai."

Paige's breath started getting loud. "You're going to try to turn me?"

Dominique said, "You can trust that I won't do anything to you that would frighten or scare you. I am actually your friend. I knew a friend of a friend of yours and I cared for her quite a bit."

Paige was confused. "Who?"

"Sarah. The girl who pulled you back from the ledge. Yes, Ms. Dalton, I know most things about you."

Paige almost doubled over. Sarah. She hadn't thought of that blue-haired girl for some time. She and Father Ferguson worked together. That's all she knew.

"She was a former nun. She joined Father Ferguson to fight us in Pittsburgh. She was sent to kill me. I thought she was funny. She didn't kill me. But I also didn't kill her. You see I have a certain fondness for humans. Or at least one."

Paige looked at this vampire, this man, and knew him. She didn't know how she knew him, but something clear and engulfing inhabited her and she suddenly knew this Dominique.

"You loved her," Paige said quietly.

Dominique raised his eyebrows and lowered them. "Well, I'll let you know. It's not easy for two kinds sworn to kill each other to come together. They may romanticize it in the movies, but the truth is, it's very hard. And the truth is, it doesn't always work out."

Paige nodded, "I understand."

He smiled, "I can see why Sarah saved you. Why Shanus saved you too."

Paige perked up. She heard the first part of Shane's name and wondered if this was all related. "Are you talking about Shane?"

"Shane? God, he's not creative," Dominique laughed. "Yes. You and him don't stand a chance if you tried."

Paige had no idea what Dominique was talking about but she raised herself to her hands and got to her feet. "I don't think you're a bad vampire. I know nothing about this, but if you have the capacity to love you must have kindness and compassion in you. When I was sick and tired and broken I saw the whole world as evil. But it wasn't."

"My dear Paige," Dominique said. "You are somehow both learned and naïve. It's a strange mix. But I appreciate it. I must tell you something, just for your own sake. To grow that naïveté to strength."

"Okay," Paige said slowly. "I don't need anyone to tell me how to grow, forgive me, but it's true."

"I ordered 'Shane' to possess you. I don't know why you took him in, but it was a mistake. He was sent to kill you and take over your soul. He knows a great deal about you. I don't know what he's told you, but it's all a lie."

Paige felt a stab of hot, fiery pain but she ignored it, kept it stuffed down. She couldn't see her feet anymore and she sharpened her vision, focusing. "He's never lied to me once. He's a man of little words."

Dominique opened his mouth and closed it. "He wanted to turn you."

"I don't know who you think he is, I don't know what he's done but I know the person who saved my life and helped rebuild my shop," Paige said. "That's not an evil person. That's not a demon. So even if he were trying to turn me, that's not him."

Dominique paused, his eyes flashing red. "You remind me of Sarah. But in ways that frustrate me."

"Dominique, I love Sarah, but I'm not Sarah. I'm my own woman. I'm Paige. And you're going to have to kill *me* if you plan to hurt anyone I care about."

Dominique stared at her hard. At first she wondered if he might kill her right on the spot, but even if he were a demonai or vampire or whatever, she wouldn't go without a fight. Now knowing he cared for Sarah, made her want to summon that blue-haired girl's energy.

"I can arrange that. Believe it," he said and walked briskly out of the room and shut her back in memory-darkness.

She fell to the floor, heaving.

If someone had told Shane a few weeks ago that he would be leading his worst nemesis to his coven to find Paige Dalton, the woman he was supposed to possess, he wouldn't have believed a moment of it. But here he was, in a century-old gray-drenched steel mill. The other members of the coven lived in various "offices" of the former mill but Dominique usually hung out in the main space watching over the traffic of his coven after he had given them possession orders. When Father Ferguson and Shane entered the space, after having speedily taken down two guards, they didn't see Dominique.

"Didn't Flora say based on his temperature or something he was in here? Her science-y compu-stuff?" Ferguson asked.

"She was just monitoring him based on his lack of body temperature and watching him as a moving coordinate," Shane explained. "It doesn't mean he's here."

"I don't understand any of that."

"You got old at 42. In your youth you get old."

"42 is not young, Shane."

"Say that to the 500 year old."

"Who looks like a 36 year old."

"Are you complimenting me, Fergie?"

"Face forward, asshole," Ferguson said and pointed his sword at the open space. He and Shane had stopped by Ferguson's place and accrued a few of Ferguson's old vampire-hunting weapons he had saved from the Vatican after they kicked him out. A crossbow, sword, several knives, and a host of rosaries and crucifixes. He hated that he shared them with Shane, but he needed his knowledge of the coven to navigate the place and Shane needed Ferguson's GodSource to fight Dominique. It was an uneasy alliance for sure.

Old furnaces, long stacks and dead gray pipes that were long done with blowing smoke jutted above them. A lingering scent of smoke and entrails of fog followed them as they walked. They scanned the hairy floors and ignored the floating groan that swept the old brown place. Long, hollow, swinging voices broke out and Ferguson looked at Shane.

"Normal?"

"Yes," Shane said. "Those are the songs of the sirens, the demonai who had been possessed but could only express themselves in song."

"It's actually kind of beautiful even though it's terrible."

"You wouldn't understand it," Shane said and grabbed his arm. "His quarters are to the left." The sirens sang on. Shane had been fighting a sinking feeling the entire day. He kept convincing himself he was going back to the coven to defeat Dominique and take over the place, or to reckon with Dominique in some way, and not save Paige Dalton. But her stupid face, in pain, bloodied, even possessed, kept flashing across his mind's eye and he felt his chest seize up and shudder just thinking about that. Useless human mind.

Shane led the way past the corridor of closed demonai rooms until he reached the end of the hall. There was one room, which used to be some tycoon's office, where Dominique resided. He rapped on the door, shut his eyes. Was he really doing this? This was insane.

Dominique immediately answered. His cold, white face and long eyelashes fluttered. He looked at Shane, then Ferguson.

"Guests! Welcome. I gather you know who I am?" His red eyes darted over their weapons. "And you came prepared!"

He raised his hands and shook them. "Yet I have nothing. Because I don't want to hurt you, dear humans." He waved them into his long, red-washed room, disturbingly empty save for a rack of swords and an empty bookcase, and they cautiously followed.

"I'm happy to see you both. Father Ferguson. It's been a while," Dominique walked over to the row of swords he usually kept in his quarters next to a long, cushioned coffin laying on the ground.

"That's my sleeping quarters. Cliched, right? But it's comfortable. I like never forgetting that I'm dead."

He waved them over to a shelf of gold, gleaming jewels and goblets. "These are my treasures. Shanus and I have been on many adventures getting these." He cut his eyes at Shane.

"Right, Shanus? Or rather 'Shane?'"

Shane blinked. There was no point in pretending anymore. "Good times."

"Remember that time we possessed those twins? They were reaching for each other. Ah, the love. Then they were killed by Father Ferguson's kind immediately afterward."

"Good times," Shane repeated and he felt that sizzle of pain he'd been feeling when he thought of Father Ferguson's Elsie or imagining Paige in danger. Father Ferguson walked forward.

"They were trying to kill innocent people. We kill your kind, no disrespect, because you are all killers."

"Are we?" Dominique grabbed a sword from his rack and pointed it at Father Ferguson. "In my day, which was Japan in the Kamakura Era, long before you all can conceive of… we would just settle things this way. In Pittsburgh, I wanted us to maintain some privacy. But look at Lias! Attacking coffee shops to find you, Shanus."

"You didn't send him?" Shane said, confused.

"Of course not. You're Shanus. I would have set Missy or someone to retrieve you. I would have gotten you myself. That Lias was always jealous of you and thought he could find your trail at Paige's, the last place you went. I didn't even know about it until the news reported her shop had been attacked by an idiot with a crossbow."

"Seems like you've got things in order here," Father Ferguson said. Dominique half-smiled at Ferguson.

"You've been excommunicated, yes? We were wondering why we haven't seen you around. And…" He strode forward and lay a hand on Ferguson's shoulder. "You say you don't have the GodSource, but we all know you lied to them. You have it quite strongly." He gripped Father Ferguson's shoulder. "So. I should be afraid of you, yes?"

Ferguson glared at him. "Yes."

"And yet I'm not," Dominique said, releasing him. He looked at Shane, and at the first time in Shane's 500 years he saw a glimmer of unadulterated rage in Dominique's eyes. "But this one betrayed me. So, he must go first."

As Dominique lunged at Shane, Shane fell out of the way and Father Ferguson blasted Dominique with a crossbow in the arm. Dominique took the blow, ripped the arrow out of his arm and kept walking toward Shane.

"That wasn't blessed, Father Ferguson," he said to the former priest. "You need to make a decision which side you want to play for. Let me guess. The good ol' Catholic Church doesn't want you anywhere near them after you defected." While Dominique looked as if he were challenging Ferguson, he came for Shane again, and Shane rolled over and grabbed a sword from Dominique's rack. They faced each other, squarely. Father Ferguson also slipped in and got a sword.

"Okay," Dominique said. "This will actually be quite fun. Two humans against a coven leader. Which means it's almost half a fair fight."

Ferguson surged at Dominique, but Dominique easily kicked him into a dresser. Ferguson tried again, this time trying to summon the GodSource, but it was acting up and Dominique, saw an opening and kicked Ferguson into his other armoire. Father Ferguson groaned, and Shane could hear the muscles in his back tear. Dominique raised his sword to finish Shane off but Shane, against his better judgment, grabbed Dominique's shoulders and brought him back to the center of the room.

"This ain't fun if we ain't riding, Dom," Shane said.

"I agree," Dominique said. "It's been a long time since we faced off."

Shane showed his sword. "We've never faced off…" Dominic smiled, his teeth tightly pressed together. "We have. Once. The man before me looks exactly like the brilliant man I possessed in Barcelona half a century ago. He was young, handsome, extremely devoted to his business and sister. A world-class man. Could be a leader someday. I knew I had to have him, turn him. But when I possessed you, it didn't turn out clean. You became something monstrous, unreal, and unfeeling. So I blocked you off from your past life and you became like a true demon. It was amazing. You were a treasure. And now. Well, I'm disappointed."

Shane felt his insides weaken but he wouldn't let Dominique see a thing. In the many years they'd been fighting together he never knew his past and never asked, thinking knowing such a thing would weaken him indefinitely. But here he was talking about a sister. He saw a girl's face, a Moor, brown like Flora. She was crying for him as she was taken away by vampires. He saw his mother's face pleading for them to save her daughter. He saw himself offer his own life in their place. Then he saw Paige out of nowhere, then Flora. Then he saw, weirdly, Father Ferguson, who he desperately hated. Then he saw the poetry reading.

"You killed my family," Shane said, simmering. "You killed them to get me."

Dominique wiped his sword with a white cloth he kept in his front pocket. "I needed you. We had to free ourselves from these systemic religions that bequeath the GodSource onto their priests and priestesses and vanquish us. They don't understand us. They don't understand we have hearts."

"I didn't have a heart," Shane said fiercely, remembering everything. He thought about passing out, but he couldn't. A pastiche of faces, the men and women he'd killed and possessed all in service to Dominique burned against his eyes and he saw flashes of black and wondered if he would be killed on the spot because he was so weak and so deserving of death. "You took my family away from me. You made me into something I wasn't."

Dominique shrugged. "And you lived eternally. You added to our coven. You never knew unhappiness because I kept reality from you. I made your life good and you're ungrateful." He gestured at Father Ferguson, "You helped us save ourselves from humans. You were ours. And yet you killed your own."

Shane was sick of talking. Now he remembered it all: how Dominique had killed his family anyway, even after promising to protect them. His body glowed orange with anger and rage and all he wanted to do was end Dominique. For his family. For Paige and Flora. For himself. He felt Father Ferguson out of the corner of his eye and felt him brace with his sword.

Shane said to Dominique, "You're not walking out of this room alive."

Dominique stepped forward lightly and pointed his sword at Shane, almost bored. "Shane, I'm already dead. Here: I have a little story to tell you. Once upon a time I met a girl. She hunted us to protect her kind. Then she met me. I tried to possess her but instead I fell in love. And she left me and died. Welcome to humanity. I had a moment, a brief moment, when I wanted to be human. To be with her. But it was impossible. I couldn't even die by her side."

"Sorry?" Shane said, growing increasingly irritated with Dominique. Now this asshole was talking about his fucking romances? He never knew Dominique to even think about humans in any way but curious disdain. But he'd received so many surprises in the past few weeks nothing surprised him anymore.

"Sounds like you're a hypocrite."

Dominique flew at Shane and Shane hurled his sword back and met Dominique's sword cleanly. Sparks flew out and Shane pressed harder, trying to get Dominique to buckle, but Dominique overpowered him and got Shane on the ground.

"Looks like I'm not the only one. You came here for Paige Dalton. I knew you would."

Shane shoved Dominique off of him and faced him. "I'm here for myself."

"I killed Paige," Dominique said simply. "It was very easy. She's beautiful and has a beautiful neck. I can see why you feel how you feel about her. I snapped that neck clean in half."

Paige. That woman. Dead.

Shane jumped up to his feet and stabbed Dominique in the side of his torso. He shoved it deeper and deeper and Dominique fell back, visibly in pain but not deterred.

"Ouch. Ouch, dear. You're angry. Yes. Get angry. That's how I felt when this nasty world took Sarah from me. That's how I felt when I was born into this terrible body, and I couldn't breathe the fresh air or feel my own blood bumping or live a life of color and mystery. That's how I felt. But here you are. Human. Without any reason. So, so weak though. For example," Dominique fiercely stabbed Shane back in the side of his torso and Shane experienced an explosion of pain. He fell to the ground, and with the bit of strength he had left, he ripped the sword somewhere out of his stomach. He was throbbing and unreal and red was slipping from him, and he realized he would probably die soon like all of the people he had killed. Like Ferguson's Elsie, the blonde girl with the puckered mouth. He shouldn't have killed her. She was sweet, like Paige. She was kind, like his sister who he was enraged he hadn't thought about for 500 years. He threw his sword over at Father Ferguson, who picked it up quickly, and faced Dominique with two swords. The GodSource finally worked, now that Father Ferguson was fired up. He came at Dominique, who dodged his blows after Shane had temporarily weakened him. Father Ferguson plunged both swords into Dominique's shoulders, which rattled him, but not for long. Dominique removed himself from Ferguson's blows.

"I honestly don't care if you have the GodSource," Dominique said. "I always admired you Father F, mostly for your connection to Sarah, but I suppose you must die tonight too."

Dominique and Ferguson viciously traded blows, lights sparking out of their swords until Dominique found an opening and stabbed Ferguson in the chest. Ferguson fell back, blood flying from his mouth. Dominique, victorious, gently removed his sword from Ferguson, leaving him with one.

"Come on, Father. Or Shane?" Dominique said, his voice soft, near tender. "You've come to avenge your race. But you can't even get up. This is so disappointing. I guess you must die looking into my eyes, rife with such disappointment."

Dominique looked up gradually and saw a woman in the door. That Paige Dalton. She was alive after all. Waves of weakening relief washed over Shane and he tried to ignore them but he was delirious with joy. She looked at bloody Shane and Ferguson, and she ran to both of them hoping to check on them. When she reached Shane, he gripped her face and yanked her down to his ear. "Get the fuck out of here," Shane said. He got halfway off of the ground. He coughed out blood. "He's going to kill you and you need to live. We've done enough that we deserve to die. Not you though. *You* have to live, Paige Dalton…"

She ran a hand over his hair. "Oh, Shane. You don't know me very well."

"How much do you know?"

"I was just debriefed on everything by Flora. And I'm still here. I still believe in you." Dominique came over and wrenched Paige off of Shane. She rolled back on the polished floor.

"Paige Dalton," Dominique said. "It would be terribly sad to kill you. I'd probably cry if I did."

She came to her feet. "You won't kill me. I know you won't. You'll try but you won't."

Dominique's eyes flashed. "You think me to be too weak, my dear."

"No. I can clearly see your heart."

"That's sweet," Dominique said. "But you're not Sarah. So, I can kill you, with much reluctance." He grabbed his sword and came at her, but Shane tackled him to the ground, pushed Dominique's face into the floor and put his forearm at the back of his neck to keep him down. He got one of his arms and twisted it behind him. Dominique would break from it easily, but he needed to get Father Ferguson's sword. It might be doomed but it would be enough time to get Paige out of the room.

"Hey, Paige," he hollered as he and Dominique wrestled like Jacob and the angel. "Get the sword. Get it to me. Then get the fuck out of here."

"Okay," Paige said, stuffing her breath back in. She ran over to Father Ferguson to grab his sword and he handed the scabbard to her.

"Oh, Father," she said. "I hope you're okay."

"Just get the sword to Shane," Ferguson said. Paige took the sword and obeyed. She started back to Shane but Dominique cleanly lunged at her and she met his blow sloppily with Ferguson's sword. They broke away from each other, stared each other down. Shane's human heart beat wildly out of his chest as he writhed on the ground. He didn't want her to be hurt, didn't want her to be hurt. Stupid he was even thinking these thoughts.

"Sweetheart," Dominique said. "This isn't about Shane. It's about you and me."

"And Sarah," Paige said, falling back. Dominique pointed the sword at her and said, "I won't kill you if you join us. Well, I'll kill you but you'll live forever with all of us."

"You don't want that for me. Or yourself." Paige said, gently. Dominique swiped at her, but she countered him. She looked at her own hands, stunned by their glowing.

Father Ferguson leaned over and yelled at Shane "She has the GodSource. Just like me."

Shane swallowed and nodded. He knew it too. Maybe he'd always known it but just chose to believe it wasn't true. For him. For her.

Dominique overheard them and he walked in a circle around Paige, pointing his sword at her neck the entire time.

"So. You have the GodSource. I always thought that idea was bullshit. That it only came from Mary's tears they found in some relic sounded pretty stupid. Didn't make any sense but that's the garbage that's been spitting out for so long. I don't think your God works that way. Or anyone's." He smiled. "Looks like I was right. But this will certainly be a more fun fight."

Dominique jumped at Paige and she dodged him. The glowing in her hands strengthened and she looked possessed herself, her face blasting light all over the cold room. She tried a few moves at Dominique and for the first time he was set aback. He stumbled backward and she parried, moved forward, slashed at him swiftly.

"Please," she said, swinging the sword, looking like they were someone else's arms. "I don't want to kill you. I really don't. I just want to save my friends"

Dominique tried to kick her but she caught his leg and got him on the ground. She threw herself on top of him and Shane expected her to deal the final blow but she raised the sword and instead put it straight against his neck.

"How can I save my friends. Tell me and I'll save your life. I know you know how. You all don't die from flesh wounds, I'm guessing."

Dominique smirked. "Both of your friends are human. They will die. And soon."

Paige stabbed Dominique in the gut, cleanly. Astonished, he sunk into the ground. She got back to her feet and said, "I'm also your friend too. I'm sorry I did that but you look like you'll recover pretty fast. Anyone who is a friend of Sarah is a friend of mine. All of you men," she swept her hand at Father Ferguson and Shane. "Need to just chill the hell out! Now, everybody is going to the hospital and after you all recover we're all going to have a movie night at Le Bean. Deal? That's what we're doing."

The men on the ground groaned. Paige, anew with the GodSource, realized she didn't need the hospital after all. She pressed her glowing hands into all of these tired men's wounds and they grew smaller.

Shane, shiny-skinned and healing, sat atop the roof of Le Bean, watching the blue-black sky. It was March and the Pittsburgh weather was still dead-cold, but he could feel a surge of warmth trickling in. He sensed the door was opening and he looked back lightly to see Paige Dalton, holding an itchy brown blanket, climbing up to join him.

"You're feeling better?" she asked. It had been a few months, and Dominique had left Pittsburgh with his vampires entirely. Father Ferguson recovered faster than Shane, most likely because of the lingering GodSource, and Shane took a longer time to heal but improved steadily. He could now move around and walk easily, but he hadn't spoken much to Paige or Flora since the incident in the steel mills. Paige had plainly acted as if it had never happened, and Father Ferguson had only come over a few times to the coffee shop, probably in the safe care of his boyfriend as he recovered.

Shane breathed out, looking at the star-specked spread above. "Why the hell do I have a second chance?" he asked no one. "I don't deserve it. I couldn't even save my family."

"What?" Paige said leaning in.

"Nothing," Shane said. He rested his head in his hand and his long hair fell forth in his eyes. He slid a short glance at her. "How do you feel?"

"Great!" she said. "As great as can be to find out my new stranger-friend actually attempted to turn me into a vampire a few months ago. And that my former priest is actually a vampire hunter. And that I've almost been killed twice in one year. But besides that ALL is totally well."

Shane chuckled. "I can tell."

Paige softened. "Shane, I don't know what you've done in the past, but we've all done things. I'm sure you could see my darkness and all that when you tried to what was the name of it?"

"Possess you."

"Yuck. Well, possess me. You saw everything. And you still saved me."

"You haven't killed as many people as I have. Or possessed them. Your life is very tame. Everybody gets depressed sometimes, suicidal ideation is very common." Paige nearly doubled over laughing and he raised an eyebrow. "That's funny to you?"

"No. You don't know a damn thing. But at least you're self-examining. That's a sign of human maturity! You should feel good about that."

Shane smacked his lips. "I don't."

Paige stared at the same sky that Shane gazed upon. She unfolded the blanket on both of their legs, and she patted his thigh gently then removed her hand.

"You're a good man, Shane. You may not feel it, but you are."

"I don't exactly aspire to goodness. I think that's a crock. Aren't you humans more complicated than good and bad?"

"Fair. Rather, you have compassion. I don't care how they brainwashed you. It's there. It'll grow. And we can do some fun work." She rubbed her hands together. "Protecting the city from vampires? Solidarity! I think we can do it."

"That sounds impossible," Shane said. He scratched his nose. This woman. "How are you this naïve?"

She winked at him, converting into that dancer who could claim any man. "Baby, I could turn you out. I'm not that naïve."

Shane's heart seized up and his eyes got huge. He tried to say something but he felt so many sensations below his belt he could barely speak. He tried a "Wha…" but she went back to staring at the sky. "A girl can dream of a fantasy future. But I want a good real one."

She edged closer to him under the blanket and his leg moved over closer to hers. It felt fine, soft, kind.

The door of the stairwell slammed open, and Flora was standing at the mouth with a pair of glasses on and her huge curls up in a topknot. "Father Ferguson's here."

"Invite him up! And hang out with us. We're just hanging." Flora's eyes flew to the blanket, and she grinned small and walked back inside. "I'll get him," she said and disappeared. A few moments later, after Shane and Paige watched the pink clouds crumble over the rippled white sky, which sank into cityspace, Father Ferguson and Flora joined them. Ferguson also saw the blanket and found a deck chair and sat a considerable distance away from them. Flora was rocking back and forth on the ledge and sang like a siren to the emerging moon.

"Can you believe there are vampires in Pittsburgh?" Flora finally said. "It's crazy. I guess the blogs were right."

"Of course there are vampires in Pittsburgh. They're everywhere," Shane said. "Don't be surprised if you see one some night."

"*Everywhere,*" Father Ferguson agreed.

"There are humans too. There's love too," Paige said. "There's also love in Pittsburgh." And they paused, regarding her, thinking she was a little foolish, a little bit strong. Then they agreed.

Commercial Break

The Day the Salt Ran Out in the City

WQED: Good morning, Pittsburgh! Apparently, we're running low on salt. The City of Pittsburgh had not anticipated the recent snowfall and did not order sufficient salt to battle the storm. Let's go out to the phone lines and see how everyone's doing.

Hi, I'm a caregiver and I literally can't get to my client. I'm literally just sitting here in front of a mound of snow. I'm literally about to literally sacrifice my life here.

I work in the hospital. What do I do? My supervisor said to just sleep in the cot. I don't want to sleep in the cot. God, I don't want to sleep in the cot.

Hi, yinz are just stupid. The suburbs have salt. We don't have salt here in Greenfield. Nothing dahn-tahn. Inconceivable. What do they think? It's going to be summer every winter? We live in PITTSBURGH. In-fucking-conceivable.

Hi. I want to talk to the person from the hospital. What do you want? DEAL WITH IT. We all have to figure out how to get back home from work.

Yo, try to get some water softener. You can melt your snow or ice. If you can find one, get it. Man, it's sooooo good. I'm in Morningside.

Are they closing the schools? Are they closing the schools? Are they closing the schools? What about Fort Cherry? Are they closing the schools?

Hi, I want to talk to the person talking about softener. What the hell is a softener? I'm using kitty litter. It works. It works good enough!

This is SO FUCKING STUPID. I can't get to my paper route, you motherfucking assholes, and you better not fucking bleep me oh now you're cutting me off and---

I think we all need to deal with this rationally. I think they do have enough salt and we're overreacting. I'm a professor at Pitt and I tell my students—

I blame the Mayor! That asshole should spread it out himself.

I'm FUCKING BACK AND YOU BETTER NOT HANG UP ON ME THIS TIME—

Hellloooooo, is this Domino's? Hi. Damn, wrong number. Helloooooo.

FUCK YOU, THE CITY OF PITTSBURGH!

We'll return to the Community Talk after this commercial break.

10

Respect the Chair

It was mid-winter and the sky had upchucked six heaving inches of snow on the narrow street in front of the row-house where Jake Yee, Lady, Stills, and I lived.

I awoke early, around 5am, my mind a-fizz with nasty thoughts. I'd recently gotten into graduate school, and I wondered if I'd be good enough, if I could survive leaving the city. I rolled off my futon onto the sleek oaken floor. I lay on the ground, glaring at the ceiling, feeling the cool of the wood on my bare legs. I hadn't told any of my friends I was leaving Pittsburgh. I wondered if starting a new life on my own was a good idea.

My door slammed open and there was Jake Yee, nearly out of breath.

"You're up," he said, his eyes heavy with the usual red from his late-night paper shift.

"You came to wake me up?" I said, shifting to my side on the floor.

"Why the hell are you sleeping on the ground?"

"Because I'm weird."

"God, you really are. Anyway. I heard a thump and just wanted to check if you were okay."

"Nah, I just voluntarily rolled off the bed to the floor to contemplate my life."

"What about it?" he said, his voice smooth as a wet pebble. He looked heavily exhausted, and he walked over to my bed and slumped on the side of it. He ran a hand through his dark hair.

"Nothing," I said.

"Nothing?" he cocked his head at me.

"Nothing."

"Okay," he said. "That's fine."

"So," he started and inched on my bed closer to me. He looked down at me, stretched out on the floor. "Listen—"

"Yeah?" I said. He narrowed his eyes at me and peered down at my small body flailed out on the floor.

"I can't talk to you seriously while you're on the floor."

"Then join me!"

"Jesus," he said and he fell down on the floorboards next to me. He rested his hands behind his head and stared at the bumps and swells in the ceiling.

"I want to ask you something. And I don't really care how you feel about Benedict. I just really want to know."

At this I shot up straight, trying to think of an excuse to leave. "I have to go to the bathroom," I said and started to get up.

"Really? You seriously have to piss RIGHT NOW?"

"Yes," I said.

"Then before you go, listen to what I have to say. It'll be quick. Then contemplate your answer in the fucking bathroom."

"I really have to go."

"Look, I want us to go out proper. Like a date. A real date. Then we can go on more dates. You see where I'm fucking going with this, Adrienne?"

I nodded.

His face got soft, gentle; he didn't look like the normal sharp-talking Jake Yee. "Okay, then."

"I'm going to the bathroom now."

Jake Yee smacked his lips. "Okay. I need to park. I left my car out in the middle of the road so I could unload the rest of the papers. When we are both done with our 'business', we're talking. And you're also going to tell me the thing that made you sleep on the floor."

I bolted to the bathroom we both shared in the hall-way of the second floor of our place. I left Jake Yee in a cloud of his own frustrations. I stood inside of the bathroom and stared at myself in the mirror. Not really feeling like looking at myself at that moment, I consid-ered taking a shower to prolong the conversation I didn't want to have with Jake Yee when I heard him cry out. I ran, practically fell down the stairs and saw the door hanging open and Jake Yee screaming at a car that was supposedly in his parking space. The Chair, a city-wide fixture that protected your spot, had been kicked over by an Oldsmobile with a California license plate. Nobody was in the vehicle, but Jake Yee was still screeching. "Respect the fucking Chair!" he said to the car and walked around the length of the vehicle, hollering at it as if it were a person. "Respect the Chair!"

He waded through inches of snow that went up to mid-thigh and grabbed his knocked over chair and walked it up the porch steps. He threw it down next to the little table with his smoking materials.

"Are you fucking serious? *California*? So. Fucking. FRUSTRATING."

Now was definitely not the time to talk to Jake Yee about moving.

"There are like no spots around here! Now I have to park at the what…gas station?" He let out a grunt. He whipped around at me.

"Don't leave. Don't go to sleep. Don't take an excruciatingly long shower. I want to talk to you."

"Just find your spot first."

"No!" he said, loudly, fully pissed off, his face red. "Adrienne, what is wrong with you? Why do you keep avoiding me whenever I just want to fucking date you? You like me! Is this just about Benedict? What the hell are you—"

"Jake, I'm moving," I finally said. He stepped back, recoiling. "I'm moving for graduate school. I love Pittsburgh. I actually truly love it. Even the fucking Chair. But I'm going to New Orleans. I've lived here my whole life, and I want to try something new. On my own."

His eyebrows flew up. He looked as if he'd been physically attacked. His face changed expressions, and I wanted to disappear from the spot right there. "Okay," he said, still in shock. Then he said, limply, "Congrats?"

We stared at each other, for a long moment, when Jake Yee's eyes drifted off and he noticed something out of the corner of his eye. A happy-mouthed, forty-yearish white guy was strolling to his car, when Jake Yee ran over to the corner of the porch, grabbed his chair and he raged down the stairs.

"Hey!" he said. "Hey, asshole! In Pittsburgh, you have to RESPECT. THE. CHAIR. That's my parking spot. I live here!"

The white man's smile dropped. "What are you doing up this late? Or this early? Shouldn't you be sleeping?"

Jake Yee shook the chair at him.

"I deliver the *Post Gazette* out the back of my fucking car," Jake Yee shot back. "In the middle of the night. Immigrant business to pay for school. You fucking gringo."

California looked back at him pityingly. "Well, that's nice. But this is my spot and there's too much snow to park anywhere else."

"It's called a shovel."

"Same to you, Chinaboy. Get the fuck back to your papers then."

At this, I retracted. This wasn't going to go well for California. Jake Yee told me that generally Americans knew a bare minimum about Asian culture, so he decided to mess with them all by playing up a stereotype to get back at them. He'd pretend he was good at math (he was horrible), and offer to tutor kids who assumed he was an academic star. Then when they'd fail, he'd laugh to himself, feeling like he got a win for The Culture. He'd also mastered exactly one amazing kung fu move that he used to ward off predators and racist people. I guessed he would be using this one single move today.

Jake Yee smiled with half of his mouth. "Chinaboy, huh? Have you ever been to China? You do know what we do there?"

California blinked. "Karate or something?"

"Exactly," Jake Yee said. "Every single kid in China has to learn kung fu. We're all trained in it and we're actually quite good."

Here we go. He'd ripped that line from Jet Li, I was pretty sure, but he was totally going to own this white boy.

California's eyes stretched big. "You're shitting me."

"Nah, no shit," Jake Yee said, strolling around his Oldsmobile. "You want to see some kung fu?"

California's eyes switched to me, then back to Jake Yee. His chest was broad and pushed out in bravado, but I could see he was wondering, wondering, if Jake Yee was telling the truth.

"I don't want to see it."

"Okay," Jake Yee smiled. "You won't see it if you move your fucking car."

At this, California's ego pumped up. "I'm not moving."

"You ever heard of the Two Wing Chun Chain punches?" Jake Yee's stretched his eyes and he leaned back, brought his fists up. He winked, "You don't want to see it. You really want to see it?"

California looked from me to Jake Yee a few more times. I stared at the face-off and a strange, jagged love filled me as I gazed at Jake Yee scowling. I looked at the flushed-faced California and Jake Yee's thin body consumed by a frayed jacket flying in the wind. My feet lifted from the night-blacked porch and the bottoms of my bare feet warmed. I closed my eyes and raised my hands. They glowed fierce, they healed and shone and woke with something sourced from God, something born in the name of the moon, and with that glowing I wrenched my hands back, rammed them forward at California. The glowing streamed over to him and blasted him hard in the belly.

He flew backwards in a long arc and slammed against the Subaru across from us. He growled, wrenched himself up. He brushed furred snow from his shoulders and ripped his eyes from me to Jake Yee. Despite me hitting him cleanly mid-belly, he was unfazed. He ignored me completely and raged toward Jake Yee as if I wasn't there. Jake Yee raised his fists and California lunged at Jake Yee and I caught California in the fucking jaw with a roundhouse kick. Loser. He collapsed, got up, fell again, struggled upwards, looked at me, finally. He cussed *bitch* then grumbled over to his car and got in painfully, gradually, because he was parallel parked into 6 inches of snow, veered out and left. Triumphant, Jake Yee turned on his heel. He stamped over to me and slapped me in the palm without looking me in the eyes and spit, "Good job. *Finally*, Adrienne." Then he grabbed his Chair.

He stomped down the porch stairs and slammed it into the space between two snow-smothered cars.

"And that's how. It. Is. Done!" he cried. "Damn, RESPECT. THE. FUCKING. CHAIR."

A white stretch of cloud skidded over the moon, and I could barely see the outline of Jake Yee's body. "So go park your car, now," I said, my voice dipping low. "Before you have to actually bring out the Two Wing Chun Chain punch."

Jake Yee turned to me. His face was pale, vulnerable, fully naked. The still-violet spread above us pulsed purple. We stared at each other, with fully denuded faces, and I could smell the old snow, and I shivered. I wanted to tell him what he wanted to hear because it was true, but I also wanted to have a fresh life, outside of Pittsburgh. I wanted to pursue my dreams, cleanly. But to break. It would be so painful.

"I'm not saying goodbye to you, Jake," I told him. "You better not say goodbye to me."

Jake looked off. He plucked a cigarette from behind his ear and reached in his pocket for a lighter. He blinked away something that could have been for me.

"Goodbye, Adrienne," he said, and took a smoke. He turned from me and all I saw was his back.

Epilogue

Eat N' Park

Jake Yee decided we should all go to Eat N' Park in August before I left to pursue graduate school. He thought it'd be a way to bring us together.

Jake Yee was still always-grumpy and oft-high, but he had also become a tad more dashing. He could woo a girl much more easily, and I let him. He wasn't my business, I told myself. Benedict also stayed in the periphery, and we longed for each other, but he was in Honduras so much it was hard to keep a relationship going even if we wanted it. Elana was becoming seriously interested in astronomy, Ferris liked collecting funny bugs and was loving geography, Dragon217 was creating new cell phone technology. Stills was in medical school at Dartmouth. Jake Yee thought we should all come together and suggested "the most depressing spot in depressing Pittsburgh" and we all told him to be more joyful, and he said, "Eat N' Park. There you go. Regional. Smiley cookies. You got it."

So, we did.

Benedict sat next to Elana and Ferris, Jake Yee and Lady sat together, and I sat with Dragon217 at the front of the table not knowing quite what to do or how to behave. It was my going away party, but I wasn't ready to say goodbye to these precious people.

"Hey," said Elana, breaking the ice. "Have you picked up the newest issue of *Vampires of Pittsburgh*? Love the art and it's really fun to read. Takes place here, there's a big vampire vs. priest fight on the Mon Wharf."

"I read it," Ferris said, kissing her head. "But I'm not into vampires."

"We should really support local art," Elana tried again, sensing the group's morale wilting.

"Who wants to read about Pittsburgh?" Jake Yee said finally. Benedict was looking straight at me, and I ignored him. Jake Yee saw us switching glances and he said, "I mean, it's fine to read about Pittsburgh but can anything cool really happen in a dead steel town?"

"Batman happened," I offered.

"She's right," Benedict said.

"I'm just saying," Jake Yee said. "Your girl's been born and raised in Pittsburgh. Bullied, thrown in corners, been exuberantly happy in this city. But would anybody care about it? When I was a kid in Shadyside my parents literally took me out and threw me in Schenley because it was so racist."

Benedict breathed out. "But isn't everywhere racist?"

Jake Yee shrugged. "This doesn't matter." He took a bite of his sandwich. I leaned back in my seat. I watched a man with an orb-belly saunter into the red-brown and beige establishment with smiley face cookies plastered on every corner and sign. I asked the waiter for a smiley cookie, and he agreed.

"You got the fucking smiley cookie, Adrienne?" Jake said, reeling his tone back in when Benedict shot him a look. "I mean come on."

"She likes those cookies," Benedict said.

"Who the fuck doesn't?" Jake said, then to me. "Which cookie did you get?"

"I'm talking," I finally said and placed my hands down on the table. I watched another couple, one with 80s fluffed-up hair and blue eyeshadow and her boyfriend, clad in Steelers gear, who was already drunk coming in with her. They sat in a booth, and I watched them order pancakes before I said,

"Hey."

"Yeah?" Elana said.

Dragon217 said, "She's really got something to say."

"Never mind," I said, shrinking back into my chair.

"No come on, talk." Ferris said.

"I came to a revelation," I said. "It's important. To me at least."

"Spit it out," Jake Yee said.

"Yeah, let's hear," said Benedict.

I watched an older man sit down and fall into his chair. He opened a Frick biography and read it earnestly. I thought about the New Years Pretzel that would come out in a few weeks at Giant Eagle, about chomping on its delicious fluffy flesh with my friends.

"*We* are Pittsburgh. Even if we don't look it. Look at us. We're just diaspora kids acting weird and stupid. In this post-industrial city. What did Reginald Eldridge say, 'I am all of them,/they are all of me, I am me, they are thee….'"

"*What* are you talking about, Adrienne?" Jake Yee said.

"I like what she's saying," Elana said.

"I guess it's fine," Ferris said.

"I like it too," Benedict said warmly. "We are Pittsburgh. Every face."

"Can't say she's wrong," Jake Yee said.

I smiled. "Exactly. That's exactly what I was talking about. Who cares if nobody cares about Pittsburgh? We do."

"Fucking nerds," Jake said, gently.

We finished my goodbye party, polishing off stickies and smiley cookies, destroying our health, but feeling warm-bellied and alive, alive, alive.

Acknowledgments

Gratefully acknowledged are the following publications, in which stories first appeared.

"The Girl in the Bomba Dress": *Latin@ Literatures*

"For August Wilson and Romare Bearden": *SOMOS Literary Magazine*

"Online" & "Neon Steel": *BIMBO: A Feminist Anthology*

"Viper/Sweet": *Hong Kong Review*

"Smoke Break": *J Journal*

"Writing Fiction": *hex literary*

This book is a love letter to youth. My deepest thanks go to those who helped me unlock memories and who encouraged me to pursue this project.

Thank you to Abba, always.

Thank you to Dr. Ross Tangedal and Cornerstone Press for believing in this project and taking it on. Thank you to editorial director Brett Hill for seeing my vision along with the entire team of talented student editors.

Thank you to my mother Sonia, the reason that I write, mi corazón. I keep going, every day, for you.

Thank you to my father, Jerry, whose amazing mind and compassion continue to mean so much to me.

Thank you to my brother, Timothy, who introduced me to superheroes as a kid. You are a superhuman, Tim.

Thank you to LaKaléa, for being both a sister and a guide.

Thank you to Jesse Biehn, for saying "Why don't you write about something that makes you happy?" You are a king.

Thank you to the entire Biehn and Ward family for supporting me always with special thanks to Carol Ward, Chris Ward, Steve Biehn, Beth Biehn, Marcia Biehn, Michael Biehn and Jennifer Blanc Biehn for rooting for me.

Thank you to Pittsburgh superstars Joe Aires, Geeta Kothari, Irina Reyn, Lynn Emmanuel, Chiwan Choi, Judeth Choi, and amazing agent Mark Tavani for pushing me forward.

Thank you to Dr. Antonio Byrd, whose fearless devotion to his craft and unabashed identity always inspire me.

Thank you to everyone at Trinity United Methodist, led by Tino and Samara Hererra, for showing me inclusivity and kindness during this process.

Thank you to Bill Campbell, who solicited me for another project that thus led to this entire collection.

Thank you to Yael Valencia Aldana, my treasured and special amiga for always being a true friend.

Thank you to Hyejung Kook, who offered so much encouragement. You are so precious to me.

Thank you to my colleagues Dr. Christie Hodgen, Whitney Terrell, Dr. John Barton, Dr. Hadara Bar-Nadav, and Michael Pritchett for lifting and supporting me. Y'all are rockstars.

Thank you to Chad Qian. For everything. You know it, you know why.

Thank you to Jackson Onose Braun, for your example. Let's always dance in the middle of a grocery store.

Thank you to Rone Shavers and Kenning JP Garcia for showing me the possibilities of speculative and experimental writing by reading your work.

To the brilliant Jen Julian, thank you for your presence, powerful writing and example.

Thank you to my students for providing endless excitement, erudition, and energy.

And most of all thank you to you, precious reader, for going on this journey with my characters. I'm forever thankful for you.

Jennifer Maritza McCauley is the acclaimed author of *When Trying to Return Home* (2023), which was a *New York Times* Editors' Choice, Best Fiction Book of the Year by *Kirkus Reviews*, and a Must-Read by *Elle, Latinx in Publishing, Ms. Magazine,* and *Southern Review of Books*. A former National Endowment for the Arts fellow, she is an assistant professor of English at the University of Missouri–Kansas City.